Stories and Activities for Teaching Children About Character
by Margaret Prien

Illustrated by Kaja Rebane and Kevin English

PAW IMPRESSIONS
PRESS

Menlo Park, California 94025

Cover and interior designer: Ingbritt Christensen
Editor: Beverly Cory

Library of Congress Cataloging-in-Publication Data

Prien, Margaret S.
        Character Links/Margaret S. Prien

Library of Congress Catalog Card Number: 99-93355

ISBN 0-9673095-0-6

How to Order
Copies may be ordered from
Paw Impressions Press
PMB 120
405 El Camino Real
Menlo Park, CA 94025
Or call 1-888-767-7797

Visit us online at www.pawimpressions.com

INTRODUCTION

There is a quote by Stephen Glenn, the author of *Raising Self-Reliant Children in a Self-Indulgent World*, that bears repeating: "In the eyes and attitudes of the parents and teachers who raise and educate them, children find mirrors though which they define themselves."[1]

We have an obligation to accept this important responsibility with every child we contact, whether as a parent, teacher, caregiver, relative, or friend. The results of our contact with a child are frequently lifelong, therefore requiring our constant attention.

"Parenting and caregiving are daily acts of courage! No astronaut stepping into outer space can rival the courage adults display in the daily act of raising or caring for young children."[2]

All human beings—whether adults, teenagers, or children—see the world not as it is, but as they are. The existing perceptions of children must be respected. Perceptions are powerful! Perceptions dictate attitude, motivation, and behavior. When someone is accused of having a "bad attitude," it is a direct result of his or her personal perceptions. The New Testament tells us, "As people perceiveth themselves in their hearts, so are they."

To develop positive perceptions, children must be in a respectful, supportive, safe, nonthreatening environment. The attitude of the parent, teacher, caregiver, relative, or friend is extremely important and critical to success. Support must be genuine and heartfelt. Children are very aware and sensitive to disingenuous individuals.

Treating children with respect and love is of primary importance. Peter McPhail states: "Children take pleasure in being treated with care and warmth; their prime source of happiness is being treated in this way. Further, when children are supported by such treatment, they enjoy treating people, animals, and even inanimate objects in the same way."[3]

All meaningful and lasting change starts on the inside and works its way out. Perceptual psychology has proven that when self-esteem is raised consciously, through positive thoughts and activities resulting in accomplishment, growth is possible.

Character Links identifies the characteristics that contribute to our perceptions of self. Perceptions are individual and unique for every child. A child's perceptions are critical in developing lifelong habits that serve him or her well. Positive perceptions allow children to realize their potential and become a positive force in our society.

Be the parent, teacher, caregiver, relative, or friend who provides the opportunity for children to incorporate Character Links in their life. Be that special person children will remember with feelings of love, gratitude, and appreciation.

---

[1] H. Stephen Glenn and Jane Nelsen, Ed.D., *Raising Self-Reliant Children in a Self-Indulgent World*, Prima Publishing, p. 71.

[2] Jane Nelsen, Ed.D., Cheryl Erwin, M.A., and Roslyn Duffy. *Positive Discipline for Preschoolers*, 2nd edition, Prima Publishing, p. 185.

[3] William Bennett and Edwin J. DeLattre, "A Moral Education," *American Educator* (Winter 1976, p. 6.)

HOW TO USE THE CHARACTER LINKS

There are 35 Character Links, appropriate for children ages 3 to 8. The Character Links are interrelated. The best way to use Character Links is to introduce them slowly, starting with Character Link #1. Incorporate each Character Link into the child's everyday experiences. There is no prescribed time for completing Character Links. Mastering the Character Links may take a year or more and the time required will vary, depending on the ages of the children.

Patience is essential. You cannot take a Character Link, work on it for a week with the children, and forget it. The principles learned are revisited every day. Once children begin to understand a Link, then it's possible to introduce the next Character Link.

Each time a child demonstrates the use of a particular Character Link, take special note of and reinforce that effort.

You cannot rush through Character Links. It is a slow process, with the need for conscious reinforcement in the classroom and at home, during rest and playtime. Assimilation of the Character Links is a process—a journey.

Character Links will give a child the foundation for a happy, productive, and satisfying life and will result in a more caring, peaceful, and loving society.

The children we touch will carry on our legacy. Our hope is that this legacy will have a meaningful and significant impact on the current generation and generations to follow.

The future of our world is in the hands of today's children.

THE CAST OF CHARACTERS:

CHADWICK—a British Shorthair
MOO-MOO—a Maine Coon
JOHN LOUIE—a svelte black Designer Cat
MISIFU—an orange Persian
LIANG—a Tonkinese
PUSHPA—a white, blue-eyed Persian
YULAN—a gray and white curly haired Selkirk

In addition to the seven cats, you'll meet Heather and Tom, their people-friends, a few other little pals:

PEPE—a small gray field mouse
LETTUCE—a freshwater green turtle
BIRDIE—a yellow bird
HEDGIE—a hedgehog
CHIPIE—a chipmunk

And now, you are about to meet them.

Contents

I AM RESPONSIBLE

1   I AM RESPONSIBLE

> Being *responsible* means being sensible, dependable, reliable, and trustworthy. Being *responsible* can also mean that you are in charge of something, or have a particular job or concern and act on it.

Chadwick loved to play. He had a toy box filled with wonderful toys: catnip mice, balls to chase, stuffed animals, toy racing cars, building blocks, Lego® pieces, and plenty of puzzles. When Chadwick started to play, he would take out just a few toys, but as time passed, he would soon have every toy in the box scattered on the floor.

One day Chadwick's mother came in the playroom and asked him to sit on her lap. She explained, "I think that you are old enough to begin to learn the meaning of responsibility. Let's discuss the toy box. When it is dinnertime, I'll remind you that it's time to put your toys away. If you forget, and I have to pick up the toys, then I will put them away for a day." Chadwick agreed that sounded fair. He loved his mother and he wanted to help out. He felt good about himself when he did the right thing.

For several days Chadwick remembered his new responsibility. Then one day his mother called him to dinner, reminding him to put away his toys. He was so hungry that he ran straight to dinner, leaving his toys scattered on the floor. After dinner, he returned to his toy box and found it empty. Then he remembered—he had forgotten to put his toys away!

Chadwick asked his mother, "How long is a day?" His mother explained that after dinner tomorrow, she would return his toys to the toy box. Tomorrow seemed so far away.

The next day Chadwick kept thinking about his toys and how much he missed them. His mother suggested that he go outside and play. It was a beautiful day. The sun was shining, and the air smelled of spring flowers. Butterflies and bees were flying in the garden. He chased a few butterflies, but he kept thinking of his empty toy box. He felt badly about not remembering to put his toys away. A day was such a long time. A bee flew by and he left it alone. He had chased one when he was a young kitten and it had stung him on his pink nose. It hurt and he had not forgotten. He liked being outside, but he couldn't stop thinking about his empty toy box. The time passed slowly. He was glad when his mother called him to dinner.

Right after dinner, the little cat ran to his toy box for a reunion with his favorite playthings. This was Chadwick's first experience in learning to be responsible. Next time, he would remember to put his toys away before dinner.

> Chadwick is **responsible** when he returns his toys to the toy box.

ACTIVITIES

Questions to promote interaction and understanding of this Character Link:

- What do you think it means to be responsible?
- Why do you think it's important for Chadwick to be responsible for returning his toys to the toy box?
- How difficult do you think it was for Chadwick to be responsible?
- What happened to Chadwick when he didn't act responsibly?
- How did you feel about what happened to him when he forgot to put his toys away?
- Who was affected when Chadwick didn't act responsibly?
- When did Chadwick start learning to be responsible?
- How will you learn to be responsible?
- When is the right time for you to begin learning to be responsible?
- What can you do to be responsible for your own personal care and safety? (Washing hands, brushing teeth, getting dressed.)
- What are some tasks that you can be responsible for?

Form a circle. Ask the children to name tasks they will be responsible for. Start by asking a child in the circle to say, "You can count on me to _____ ."

If you were responsible for a plant, what are some important things to remember to do?

If you were responsible for a goldfish, what are important things to remember to do?

Responsibility always goes with a privilege. What is a privilege? A privilege is a special right. An example would be the right to see a movie in a theater. When you go to a movie, you have the responsibility to sit in your seat and not talk during the movie.

Who can share a privilege that you have been given? What responsibility went with the privilege you were given? (Examples of privileges might be going to a favorite restaurant, going to an amusement park, visiting a discovery museum, visiting the zoo, or going to the library for books.)

What happens when you are given a privilege and don't act in a responsible way? Would anyone be willing to share something that happened when you were given a privilege and you didn't act responsibly?

(You might give an example of an adult privilege. When you are given a driver's license to drive a car, you have the responsibility of obeying rules—like stopping at red lights and stop signs. If you don't, you are given a ticket. If you are given several tickets, your driver's license may be taken away. You lose the privilege of driving an automobile.)

2

I AM RESPECTFUL

2   I AM RESPECTFUL

> Being *respectful* means showing a high regard
> or consideration for someone or something.

Chadwick's grandmother had lived a long time. Her fur wasn't as plush and velvety as it had once been. She had to wear eyeglasses when she read stories. Her fur was thin in places and her skin was loose in other places—like under her chin and tummy. She moved slowly and had to sit in a chair because she was no longer comfortable sitting on the floor. Grandma Cat had lived many, many years and had so many experiences that now she was very wise. She shared her thoughts with Chadwick, and that made him feel important.

When he was younger, Chadwick spread out his games on the floor. Grandma Cat liked to play with him, but it was difficult for her to get up and down. Now, out of respect for her needs, Chadwick sets up his games on the kitchen table.

When he was younger, Chadwick got so excited when Grandma was reading a story to the kittens that he frequently interrupted. He learned that this wasn't respectful behavior. It wasn't respectful to Grandma Cat, and it wasn't respectful to the other kittens trying to listen to the story. Now, because he has learned to be respectful, he waits until the story is over before asking questions.

Grandma tires easily and sometimes drops off for a catnap where she is sitting. If Chadwick is tired, he crawls quietly in her lap and has a catnap too. He likes being close to her. If he chooses to play, Chadwick has learned to tiptoe through the room and talk softly when Grandma is napping in the chair.

Grandma Cat brings books and toys and special treats when she visits. Once when he was a very little kitten, Chadwick had looked in Grandma's suitcase when she wasn't in the room. His curiosity got the best of him. However, when his mother stepped in the room, she was not pleased. "Chadwick, what are you doing?"

Chadwick replied, "I'm just looking to see what Grandma brought." His mother had a very long conversation with him about respecting the privacy of others. Now, he wouldn't think of looking through someone else's things.

When Grandma visits, she also likes to spend time talking to Chadwick's mother. At times Chadwick feels very impatient with this situation, because he would really like Grandma all to himself. However, Grandma explained to Chadwick that his mother was her own "little kitten" many years ago. He has learned to be respectful and not demand attention when Grandma and his mother are talking together.

When Grandma leaves, it's a sad occasion. Chadwick wishes that she could always be at his home. He knows that Grandma loves him. She always treats him in a respectful manner, even when his behavior hasn't been the best. It makes him feel good when she tells his mother, "Chadwick is such a respectful kitten."

> Chadwick shows that he is **respectful** of his grandmother when he tries to be very quiet while she is napping.

ACTIVITIES

Questions to promote interaction and understanding of this Character Link:

- How does Chadwick's behavior show that he is respectful of his Grandmother?
- When is the right time to learn to be respectful?
- How do you think Grandma Cat would have felt if she had seen Chadwick looking through her suitcase?
- How do you think Chadwick felt after his mother talked to him about respecting privacy?
- How difficult is it for you to remember not to interrupt?
- What are some of the things that you can do to show respect?
- When is it important to be respectful?
- How difficult is it to not always be the center of attention?
- How important are manners?
- What role do manners play when you are being respectful?

Form a circle and have the children repeat three times: "If we want respect, then we must learn to be respectful."

How do we show respect for someone else's privacy? Start with the first child and continue around the circle. (One suggestion could be, to knock before entering a room when a door is closed. Another suggestion is to ask permission before touching something that belongs to another.)

When your mother is talking on the telephone, how can you get her attention in a respectful way?

If the teacher is talking and you want to say something, how can you do this and also be respectful? (One example might be to wait until the teacher has finished talking.)

Go around the circle asking the children to give examples of when they behaved nicely and when they have spoken nicely.

When you remember to say "please" and "thank you" to your mother and father, your brothers and sisters, and your teacher, how do they react to you?

Another part of being respectful is learning to be tolerant. What does the word *tolerant* mean to you? Being tolerant means respecting other people's differences. Differences can be physical differences: the color of hair, the color of skin, how big or small someone is, or how someone walks or talks. Being tolerant can also mean respecting the beliefs of others that differ from your beliefs.

Being *tolerant* of other children's differences is very important. Teasing, or making fun of children who look different, talk or act differently, or believe something that you do not believe, is *not being respectful*. Share examples of teasing that you have recently heard. What could you do to stop such behavior?

3

I AM RESOURCEFUL

3   I AM RESOURCEFUL

> Being *resourceful* means being good at finding solutions
> to difficult situations and problems.

The kitten had been driven in a car out to the middle of nowhere and left beside the road on a cold, rainy day. She sat in the tall, wet grass, wondering where she was and why this had happened to her. She missed her mother. She found herself in a frightening situation.

"I need to find someone to take care of me," she thought, "but first, I need to find a house. I need to start walking and keep walking until I find a house." She was a resourceful little kitten who knew that just sitting in the wet grass crying wasn't going to solve her problem. She started walking. Her little legs were short and walking through the tall grass was difficult. She kept walking until she was exhausted. The first night, she found shelter under an overhanging rock and fell asleep.

Awakening at dawn, the kitten started walking again, searching for food and shelter. Hour after hour, she kept on walking. Her paws were sore, her fur wet and matted, but she continued her search.

The kitten had been walking for several hours when she came upon a glass structure—almost like a house—and its door was ajar. The space was just wide enough for her to squeeze through. This place was warm and toasty inside. It felt so good. All around her, she saw the most beautiful flowers, all growing in small individual pots. She curled up in the middle of

the flowers and fell fast asleep. She was exhausted from her journey.

The kitten awakened when the door opened and a young man entered the glass structure. She was frightened. She started to run, but the young man scooped her up and held her lovingly in his arms. "You must like my beautiful orchids!" he said. He looked at her wet and matted fur and her sore paws. "You've been doing a lot of walking. I'll bet you're hungry. I'll get you something to eat."

By persevering, the kitten had found a house—a glass one—and sure enough, someone to take care of her. The kind man's name was Tom.

However, there was a problem. Tom already had two cats, and he couldn't keep a third kitten. He knew that this abandoned kitten needed a good home, so Tom did some resourceful thinking. He could take her to an animal shelter, but if he did that, he couldn't be sure that someone kind would take her home. Then he thought of his neighbor, but his neighbor had two large dogs, so that wouldn't be the best home for a frightened kitten. Suddenly, Tom said out loud, "I'll call Heather."

As the kitten lapped warm milk from a saucer, she overheard Tom talking on the phone. "Heather," he said, "I have the most beautiful Maine Coon kitten. I found her in the greenhouse. Obviously, she's been abandoned. Would you be willing to adopt her?"

Heather came over immediately. She looked at the kitten, fell in love with her, and named her Moo-Moo.

Because of Moo-Moo's resourceful behavior, she had survived. Because of Tom's resourceful behavior, he found a wonderful person to adopt the kitten. Moo-Moo became a valued member of Heather's household.

In the beginning, a bad thing had happened to the little kitten because of the actions of a very unkind and thoughtless person. Despite this, Moo-Moo had the courage and perseverance to search for food and shelter. She discovered that she was worthy of love when she felt the love and compassion that Tom and Heather showed for her. There was both good and bad in her world. By being resourceful, Moo-Moo had overcome the bad and lived to celebrate the joy and love surrounding her.

> When Moo-Moo kept walking in the rain and cold to find shelter, she was being **resourceful**.

ACTIVITIES

Questions to promote interaction and understanding of this Character Link:

- What does it mean to be resourceful?
- How was Moo-Moo resourceful in the story?
- Why was it important for Moo-Moo to learn to be resourceful?
- What were the rewards for Moo-Moo for being resourceful?
- When is it most important to be resourceful? (When you find yourself in a new situation or confronted with a problem or difficulty.)
- Why was it important that Tom be resourceful?
- What was Tom's reward for being resourceful?
- What did Moo-Moo learn about the good and bad in her world? (The bad was the unconscionable act of being abandoned beside the road. The good was discovering that she was valued and worthy of love. The good was also the compassion shown by both Tom and Heather.)
- Who showed courage in the story?
- Who showed perseverance in the story?
- Who showed love and compassion in the story?

Form a circle. Ask each child to name a situation in which it is important to be resourceful. Examples:

- If there is a fire, what is important to know? How to escape from the fire. How to call the fire department. How to tell how close the fire is. How to break a window to get outside, if you can't get to a door. How to proceed when there is smoke filling a room or hall. (Keep your head close to the floor.)
- If there is a medical emergency, how do you get help? What number do you call?
- If you are lost, what action can you take? Where do you go for help? Why is it important to be able to spell your first and last name? How important is it to know your telephone number? What else is it important to know? (Your parents' names, your address.)

Being resourceful is also an important part of school. Ask the children to name something that they would like to learn more about. Help them decide what the first step might be in finding information on that subject. Assist the children in learning to be resourceful.

4

I AM TRUSTWORTHY

4 I AM TRUSTWORTHY

> Being *trustworthy* means being honest and reliable,
> someone that people can depend on.

Heather saw the jet-black kitten in a cardboard box as she entered the grocery store. The sign read, "Please adopt me!" She had adopted Moo-Moo just a few months earlier. Every day when she left for work, she knew that Moo-Moo would be lonesome staying home alone. Adopting this little black kitten to be Moo-Moo's playmate could be the answer. She picked up the kitten, tucked him inside her coat, and took him home. She named him John Louie.

As a kitten, John Louie was a terror. He jumped and chased everything that moved. Every time Moo-Moo moved her tail, John Louie would try to catch it and then bite it. When Moo-Moo walked around the house, he would jump on her back and ride along. Moo-Moo tolerated his behavior. She was happy to share her days with this new kitten.

John Louie found spiders, crawling insects, and flies a challenge to catch. But the greatest attraction of all was Birdie. Whenever Birdie moved in her cage, John Louie wanted to capture her. He tried to climb the bird stand, but it was too smooth and he couldn't hold on. He then climbed nearby shelves until he was higher than Birdie. From this position, he would jump onto the top of Birdie's cage. The cage would teeter and tip, dumping John Louie to the floor.

Heather frequently talked to John Louie about his behavior, reminding him that he must develop an awareness of Birdie's need to feel safe and secure. Birdie was a member of the household and John Louie had to be respectful of her.

Heather suggested that John Louie take ten minutes every day to visualize being a friend of Birdie. She knew that John Louie could change his behavior if he first changed the picture in his mind and started seeing Birdie as a friend instead of something to capture. Very slowly and with much effort, the little black kitten worked at changing his behavior.

Heather rewarded John Louie's good behavior with cat treats and special time with her. She bought him catnip mice, catnip-stuffed veterinarians, balls with bells in them, and even a wand toy with feathers on the end. Although he wasn't permitted to chase the feathers on Birdie, chasing the feathers on the wand as Heather waved it was fine.

John Louie enjoyed his special time with Heather. He continued picturing in his mind that he was Birdie's friend, and slowly he could see his attitude changing. After John Louie had been respectful of Birdie for a very long time, Heather could see that he was trustworthy. She rewarded him with anchovy popcorn. It was delicious.

John Louie's good behavior continued. Heather decided it was time to open the door of Birdie's cage. Birdie was wary, but finally she ventured from her cage to sit on the perch near the cage door. John Louie made no further attempts to catch her. Birdie gradually began to trust John Louie, spending more and more time outside her cage.

John Louie had slowly won Birdie's trust.

John Louie knew that he was trustworthy. He had also learned about the power of picturing something positive in his mind to help change his behavior. He would continue to picture goals in his mind. It was a skill he would use the rest of his life.

> John Louie is **trustworthy** when Heather can trust him not to chase Birdie.

ACTIVITIES

Questions to promote interaction and understanding of this Character Link:

- What does it mean to be trustworthy?
- Why was it important for John Louie to learn to be trustworthy?
- When did John Louie start to learn to be trustworthy?
- How did John Louie learn to be trustworthy?
- Why was Birdie frightened of John Louie?
- What changes in John Louie's behavior started building trust for Birdie?
- How did Birdie learn to trust John Louie?
- What helped John Louie the most while he worked to change his behavior toward Birdie?
- How did Heather encourage John Louie to learn to be trustworthy?

Form a circle and ask the children to name someone they believe is trustworthy. Ask, "What makes you think this person is trustworthy?"

Have the children name the qualities that help make someone trustworthy. For example:

- Doing what you say you will do.
- Being consistent in your behavior.
- Being dependable.
- Being honest.
- Telling the truth.

Ask the children to name one situation in which they believe that they are trustworthy.

Trust is earned. To demonstrate this, have each of the children work with a partner. Tie a scarf over the eyes of one child. Have the partner lead the blindfolded child to a designated area in the room. Reverse roles. Ask the children how they felt about their partner when they were blindfolded. What did they learn about trust?

Ask the children to name a way in which they would like to become trustworthy. For example:

- Feeding a pet.
- Caring for a pet by setting a time each day to play with it.
- Respecting the property of others.
- Being responsible for their behavior.
- Being friendly to others.
- Being willing to help others.
- Remembering to use manners when working with others.
- Being a good friend.
- Being respectful of others.

Help the children develop a plan to be successful in the goal they have chosen.

- What steps can you use that John Louie used?
- What are some additional ways to accomplish your goal that John Louie didn't use?
- Heather gave John Louie encouragement. Who can offer you encouragement?

5

I AM HONEST

5   I AM HONEST

> Being *honest* means telling the truth.

Misifu enjoyed doing helpful things for her mother. One day she saw dishes in the sink and decided to wash them to surprise her mother.

Standing on her stool, Misifu turned on the water. She poured soap into the sink and watched as the soap bubbles formed. They were iridescent and beautiful. They kept growing and growing and growing, spilling over the sides of the sink and onto the floor. She shut off the water. There were bubbles everywhere.

Misifu reached into the sink. The dishes were difficult to find because there were so many bubbles. She reached to the bottom and found a plate. By then her paws and arms were covered with soapsuds. Everything was very slippery. She carefully washed the plate and rinsed off the bubbles. Then, on the way to the draining rack, the plate slipped from her sudsy paws, fell to the floor, and broke— making a terrible racket. It frightened her!

Misifu jumped off her stool and ran to hide behind a chair. She was afraid that her mother would be terribly upset. The plate was one of her mother's favorites. What could she tell her mother? She could always blame her friend, Pepe the mouse.

She could say that he ran across the counter and knocked the plate out of her paws. But Pepe was a very good friend. She didn't want to get him in trouble. That wouldn't be fair to him.

Just then Misifu's mother walked into the kitchen. Seeing the broken plate on the floor and all the soapsuds, she asked, "Why, what happened here?"

Misifu slowly came out from behind the chair. Summoning all the courage she had, she cried, "It's my fault. I broke it!" The worst was over; she had honestly answered her mother's question.

Her mother picked her up and held her. "Thank you for being honest, Misifu. I know how difficult it can be to tell the truth when you know that someone may be upset with you. The plate was one of my favorites. I also know that you were trying to be helpful. Your being honest is more important to me than my favorite plate. In your heart, you can feel good about yourself, because you know that you've done the right thing by being honest."

Then Misifu's mother kissed her on her little pink nose and together they cleaned up the mess.

> When Misifu said, "I broke the plate," she was being **honest**.

ACTIVITIES

Questions to promote interaction and understanding of this Character Link:

- What does being honest mean?
- Why was Misifu frightened when the plate fell to the floor and broke?
- What did she do when she saw the broken the plate?
- What would you have done if you were Misifu?
- Why is it important for Misifu not to blame Pepe?
- How would Pepe feel if Misifu fixed the blame on him?
- What would happen to their friendship?
- How would Misifu feel if she had blamed Pepe?
- How did Misifu feel when she told her mother she had broken the plate?
- Why does it take courage to be honest?
- How did Misifu's mother reinforce the importance of being honest?
- How did Misifu feel when she helped her mother clean up the mess?

Why is it important to tell the truth even when you think that the person will be upset?

Each time you do something that you know is right, how do you feel about yourself?

If you found money that didn't belong to you, what would you do? What are the choices you could make?

Why is it dishonest to take something that doesn't belong to you?

When your feelings are hurt, why is it important to be honest and share that hurt with someone?

Suppose that one time you weren't honest, and you didn't tell the truth when someone asked you a question. What could you do now to make it right? What are some possible solutions?

Why does being honest build trust?

6

I HAVE CHOICES
CHOICES HAVE CONSEQUENCES

6 I HAVE CHOICES
CHOICES HAVE CONSEQUENCES

Having a *choice* means getting to decide what to do, or getting to pick one thing over another. *Consequences* are the things that happen as a result of something you do.

Chadwick loved to sharpen his claws on the living room chair. There was a corner of the chair that he found particularly appealing. His mother had told him on several occasions not to do this. However, the pleasure Chadwick found in doing this made him forget his mother's words.

One afternoon as Chadwick was sharpening his claws on his "special place" on the chair, his mother walked into the room. "Chadwick, STOP sharpening your claws on the chair." Chadwick stopped and looked down at the floor. He knew he wasn't allowed to do this.

Chadwick's mother invited him to sit in her lap while she talked to him. "Chadwick, you have choices to make, and I want you to fully understand the consequences of your decisions. In this situation, you can make two possible choices. You can make the choice to refuse to give up sharpening your claws on the chair. The consequence will be that you'll have to spend most of your time outdoors where you can't bother the chair. It's beautiful outside right now, but the rainy season is coming, and it can get very damp and cold out there. What is more important, I think that you will be very lonely if you make this choice."

Chadwick looked sad, but his mother still had more to say. She told him, "Another choice is to give up the chair and find something more appropriate for sharpening your claws. You seem to be having difficulty making this choice. Why is the chair so attractive to you?"

Chadwick replied, "When I sharpen my claws on the chair, it helps me pull the old part of my claw off. It feels better than anything else—the wooden scratching post doesn't work as well, and neither do the outdoor trees."

His mother was silent for a moment. Then she said brightly, "I have an idea. Let's go to the pet shop and try different scratching posts. See if you can find one that feels as good as the living room chair." Chadwick was doubtful, but agreed to go to the pet shop with his mother.

At the pet shop, a cat very much like Chadwick listened to the problem. He suggested trying several scratching posts, each covered with a different fabric. Chadwick tried two scratching posts, but they didn't feel as good as the chair. However, there was one more post to try. He stretched to his full height and began scratching the material. He closed his eyes and imagined he was using the chair. The fabric felt wonderful. He could hardly believe it.

On the way home, Chadwick thanked his mother for suggesting the visit to the pet shop. His mother replied, "When you're young, it's sometimes difficult to think of all the possible choices. That's why it's important to discuss your problems with someone who can help you think of a choice that may solve your problem."

Chadwick's choice of finding a substitute for the living room chair had the consequence of allowing him to remain indoors with his family. He would keep cozy and warm, and still be near his wonderful toy box.

> When Chadwick makes the **choice** to use a new scratching post instead of the chair, the **consequence** is that he can remain indoors.

ACTIVITIES

Questions to promote interaction and understanding of this Character Link:

- What does having a choice mean to you?
- What does the word *consequence* mean to you?
- Why is it so important to understand that choices have consequences?
- What is the best thing that can happen when you make good choices in life?
- What are some bad things that can happen when you make unwise choices?
- How do you learn from making poor choices?
- How did Chadwick learn about choices?
- How did Chadwick learn about consequences?
- How do you learn to make better choices?

Have the children repeat the following:

Character Links, Character Links,
There seem to be so many!
But master one and then go on
And soon you'll master many.

Form a circle. Each child takes a turn by naming one choice and its consequence. Positive or negative choices are welcomed. Examples of choices:

- Not putting toys away.
- Forgetting to put your coat on when it's cold outside.
- Not eating your dinner.
- Eating healthy foods.
- Forgetting to wash your hands.
- Brushing your teeth.
- Finding something and taking it to the lost and found.
- Spending time each day with your pet.
- Using good manners, like saying "please" and "thank you."

When we make choices, we may not always know the consequence of our choice. When you don't know, how can you explore what the possible consequences might be?

Where can you ask for help to avoid choices that don't serve you well?

How can you help someone else make better choices?

7

I EVALUATE MY EXPERIENCES AND LEARN FROM MY MISTAKES

7 I EVALUATE MY EXPERIENCES AND LEARN FROM MY MISTAKES

> To *evaluate* means to examine something in order to judge its value. *Experiences* are the things you do or see, the things that happen to you. To *learn* is to gain some knowledge that you can apply to new situations.

When John Louie was a young kitten, before he was adopted by Heather, he lived near a busy street. He heard over and over from his mother to always wait for the WALK sign and to look both ways before stepping into the street. She told him, "Many cats are hit by cars when they're careless. I don't want anything to happen to you. I love you too much."

One afternoon John Louie had gone exploring, when he realized it was getting late and he must get home before dark. He had three streets to cross. The first two had traffic signals. John Louie carefully waited for the WALK sign before crossing these streets.

The third street had no light. He was almost home. John Louie had only to cross this street, and then he could walk in his front door. He was so anxious to be home that he looked only *to the left* before he dashed into the street. He forgot about looking *right*. Suddenly, he heard brakes squealing and saw the bumper of the car from the corner of his eye. He made it to the curb by a whisker. His heart was pounding. He was so frightened that he started to tremble.

His mother heard the screeching brakes of the car and hurried to the front door. When she opened the door and saw John Louie trembling on the sidewalk, she was so relieved that he wasn't hurt. She ran to the sidewalk, scooping him up in her arms. The man in the car stopped to see if the small black kitten had made it safely to the sidewalk. She thanked him for his concern.

John Louie's mother carried him into the house and sat down, cuddling him in her lap. Slowly he stopped trembling. When his heart was no longer thumping in his chest, she said, "John Louie, we've talked about being careful crossing the street. Please tell me what happened."

Slowly he told her how careful he had been returning home, until he came to his own street. "When I crossed the street, I looked to the left, but I forgot to look to the right," said John Louie.

"I am so glad that you didn't get hit by the car," his mother said. "You have just learned a very important lesson." John Louie agreed. It had been such a terrifying experience that he would never again forget to look both ways.

John Louie was almost hit by a car, and when he **evaluated his experience**, he **learned from his mistake** to be more careful crossing the street.

ACTIVITIES

Questions to promote interaction and understanding of this Character Link:

- What experience did John Louie evaluate?
- What did he learn from his experience?
- Why was it important for John Louie to evaluate his experience?
- How did John Louie's mother treat him when he made a mistake?
- Why was it important to John Louie that his mother responded this way?
- How will John Louie apply what he has learned in new situations?
- When you don't evaluate experiences, what are you apt to do?
- Why are mistakes important? (If you weren't trying new things, you would never make a mistake. So, a mistake means that you are trying and taking risks.)
- If John Louie had never left his house, would he have learned as much about the importance of looking both ways before crossing the street?
- Why is it important to apply what we know in real-life situations?
- When do you think John Louie first started learning from his experiences? (Suggestions: When he first began to walk? When he first lapped water from a saucer? When he first began to eat solid food? When he first wandered a short distance from his mother?)

Form a circle and repeat:

Character Links, Character Links,
There seem to be so many!
But master one and then go on
And soon you'll master many.

Would any of you be willing to share an experience that you learned something from?

This activity is appropriate for children five years and older.

Manners are polite ways of behaving or acting. We're going to play a game. I am passing out purple and green colored cats in envelopes. When you get your envelope, peek inside and see the color of the cat. Don't show the cat to anyone else. Do you all know the color of your cat?

Now we are going to go around the circle. Each person is going to compliment the next one. When you hear someone compliment you, if you have a purple cat in your envelope, you will say, "Thank you." If you have a green cat in your envelope, you will say nothing.

The leader starts by turning and paying a compliment to the child on the right. The child must respond according to the color of the cat in his or her envelope. Continue around the circle.

To illustrate the importance of evaluating experiences, let's share our feelings about this activity. How did you feel when someone responded, "Thank you"? How did you feel when your compliment was met with silence? How might you change your behavior as a result of this experience?

8

I AM NEEDED, VALUED, AND IMPORTANT

8   I AM NEEDED, VALUED, AND IMPORTANT

Being *needed* means having qualities that are important to others. Being *valued* means being precious and useful to someone. Being *important* means you have great value and meaning.

Rosalva was walking to the garden and invited Misifu to join her. Misifu enjoyed adventures with Rosalva. At the garden, Misifu saw flats of plants from the nursery and another box filled with seed packets. Rosalva asked, "Will you help me, Misifu? I'll never get the garden planted without your help."

Misifu replied, "I'd love to." It was a perfect spring day for garden work. The sunshine was warm, and a gentle breeze was blowing.

"First," said Rosalva, "we'll put in the tomatoes and squash plants." Misifu sat and watched Rosalva as she tapped a stake at one end of the garden and a second stake at the opposite end. Rosalva ran a string between the two stakes. Rosalva picked up Misifu and showed her what would be most helpful. She asked Misifu to dig a hole in the dirt the depth of her foreleg, then walk twelve paw prints down the string. There, she could dig the next hole. The holes would then be the correct distance apart.

Misifu loved to dig holes. She sometimes got in trouble for digging holes where she shouldn't be digging them. This was great fun. The dirt flew. Misifu quickly moved down the row, twelve paw prints between holes. Rosalva followed her, placing a plant in each hole. Then Rosalva went back and filled in the dirt around each plant, being careful not to hurt the young leaves. Misifu loved to pack the dirt by pouncing on it with all four paws. Then Rosalva came along with a large watering can to water each plant.

The next task was planting the seeds. Rosalva made a string line as a guide for Misifu. This time she asked Misifu to dig the trench one paw-width across, and half a paw-width deep. Rosalva planted seeds for lettuce, radishes, parsley, spinach, carrots, and catnip. She planted each type of seed in a separate row. Gently they covered the seeds, and Misifu walked down the rows to pack the dirt. Rosalva followed with the large watering can, sprinkling each row of seeds.

It was late when they finally finished. They washed hands and paws and collapsed in a comfortable chair. Misifu knew she had played an important role. Her efforts were valued and appreciated. Life was "purrfect."

> Misifu felt **needed, valued, and important** when Rosalva asked her to help plant the garden.

ACTIVITIES

Questions to promote interaction and understanding of this Character Link:

- How did Misifu get involved in planting in the garden?
- Why did Misifu say yes to the invitation to join Rosalva?
- How did Rosalva make it possible for Misifu be helpful?
- What did Rosalva ask Misifu to do that the little cat really enjoyed?
- What talent did Misifu have that Rosalva encouraged?
- How did Misifu feel about her contribution in planting the garden?
- Why is it important to Misifu to help?

Form a circle and ask the children to repeat:

Character Links, Character Links,
There seem to be so many!
But master one and then go on
And soon you'll master many.

Make a list of tasks at home and at school where children feel they are capable of helping. Suggestions:

- Picking up toys.
- Cleaning up messes that they have made.
- Sweeping the floor.
- Dusting.
- Vacuuming chair cushions.
- Setting the table.
- Putting dishes in the dishwasher.

- Putting books back on the bookshelf.
- Feeding the goldfish.
- Pulling weeds in the garden.
- Planting seeds in the garden.
- Digging holes for small plants in the garden.
- Brushing teeth without reminders.
- Washing lettuce and tearing it into pieces for a salad.
- Setting the table.
- Hanging clothes in the closet.
- Folding small clothing.
- Being a parent's helper.
- Being a teacher's helper.
- Smiling and being friendly.

Invite the children to participate in a five-minute cleanup of the classroom. Ask them to clean the area right around them. This might mean putting blocks away, putting trash in the wastebasket, wiping up spills, putting playdough in containers, and returning dress-up clothing to a trunk. Set the timer. After the timer rings, ask the children to share their feelings about the result.

Ask, "How was it possible to accomplish so much in such a short time?"

9

I ENJOY LEARNING

9 I ENJOY LEARNING

> To *enjoy* means to get pleasure from something.
> *Learning* means gaining new knowledge and skills.

Chadwick enjoyed learning. Every day he found out many new things. Some of the things he learned were from mistakes or "happenings." Happenings were things that turned out differently than you thought. There were some wonderful happenings that made learning exciting and fun. There were also some happenings that weren't quite so wonderful. Even when Chadwick thought that some happenings were upsetting, he always learned from them.

One morning Chadwick was in art class. He was making a picture of the outdoors, and up in one corner the sun was shining. He had just painted the sun yellow. Now he was using a bigger brush to paint the sky blue. With one big sweep, he accidentally painted over part of the sun. Much to his surprise, the sun turned green. What happened? He wasn't even using green paint! He had only blue paint on his brush.

He called Miss Mary over to help him. Miss Mary was Chadwick's teacher, and he thought that she knew everything. He explained to Miss Mary what he had done. She smiled and said, "That's wonderful! You've discovered something all by yourself."

Chadwick frowned. He didn't think that it was so wonderful. His beautiful yellow sun had turned green on one side. Miss Mary said, "Tell me again. Exactly how did this happen?"

Chadwick repeated that he had painted the sun yellow. Then when he painted the sky blue, he had accidentally painted over part of the sun and it had turned green. Miss Mary asked, "Why do you think that the sun turned green?"

Chadwick thought and thought. Then he smiled before he answered. "When you paint blue over yellow, it makes a new color—the color green!"

"How can you use what you just learned?" Miss Mary asked.

Chadwick responded, "If I have two colors, blue and yellow, and I want green, all I have to do is mix them together."

Miss Mary continued, "I know it must feel really good to learn new things all by yourself. I can tell by your smile that you are happy."

Chadwick was so excited. He couldn't wait to mix other colors to see the results. There's something very special about discovering something all by yourself. Learning was exciting.

> Chadwick **enjoyed learning** when he discovered that combining yellow and blue made a new color—green.

ACTIVITIES

Questions to promote interaction and understanding of this Character Link:

- Why did Chadwick enjoy learning?
- Why do you enjoy learning?
- What "happening" took place while Chadwick was painting?
- How did Chadwick respond when his "happening" took place?
- When did he ask for help?
- After he asked Miss Mary for help, what did Chadwick learn?
- Why was Chadwick excited about what he learned?
- How was Chadwick going to use what he had learned?

Form a circle. Ask the children to share something they have learned, especially something they are glad to have learned. (If the children are having difficulty, suggest that they have learned to wash their hands, brush their teeth, put their toys away, talk, use the bathroom, count with numbers, identify shapes, and so forth.) Continue around the circle.

Learning often starts with wondering about something. Ask the children to complete the following sentence. "I wonder what would happen if _____?"

Encourage experimentation by passing out three colors of playdough. What will happen if you mix two or more colors? Encourage guessing what the outcome will be, then mix them.

- What will happen if I mix black with any color?
- What will happen if I mix white with any color?

What is it about learning that makes you feel good? What is it about mastering a skill or learning information that makes you feel good? List as many of the good feelings associated with learning as possible.

What feelings do you experience when you have difficulty learning or understanding something? List as many feelings as possible.

When you experience feelings of frustration, disappointment, discouragement, anger, or fear, what can you do? What are some of the choices that will allow you to feel better and solve a problem? (Among the choices, one of the most important is being willing to ask for help.)

What can you do if someone says to you something like this: "You're stupid. How come you're so dumb? You're not smart enough to learn! Won't you ever learn?! How many times do I have to tell you!?"

Sometimes things are said about you that, deep inside, you know are not true. What can you do? You can say to yourself, "That's not true! I am capable. I am continuing to learn."

10

MY ENERGY AND ENTHUSIASM INSPIRE OTHERS

10 MY ENERGY AND ENTHUSIASM INSPIRE OTHERS

> *Energy* means the strength or eagerness to work or do things. *Enthusiasm* means a feeling of excitement and great interest. To *inspire* means to stir the mind, feelings, or imagination of others.

Pushpa was a bundle of energy. She thought up wonderful games and adventures. She had a marvelous way about her. She had a loving attitude that was both encouraging and inviting. When she invited others to participate in field trips and activities, the other kittens responded to her suggestions with enthusiasm. It was so much fun being with her. Everyone wanted to participate.

Sometimes Pushpa led field trips to find and name birds. On these trips, the kittens learned to recognize the songs of many birds. It was great fun seeing who would be the next kitten to find a new bird. Pushpa organized similar trips to find bugs and butterflies. Everyone learned the names of the flowers that attracted butterflies. Smelling the flowers was an additional bonus.

On other occasions, Pushpa encouraged the kittens to make their neighborhood a better place to live. Together they picked up paper with their claws and took cans and bottles to the recycling center. They pulled weeds from the community catnip patch. They visited cats at the local veterinary clinic, spreading love and reassurance.

Pushpa gave extra encouragement when she suggested they visit the Home for Aged Cats. Some of the kittens were afraid of older cats—their fur looked funny, thin and sparse in places, and they had a lot of folds and wrinkles. Whatever would they say to someone so old? Pushpa smiled and said, "Remember that one day you, too, will be an older cat. Treat the cats just the way you would like to be treated. You'll find they have wonderful stories to tell and experiences to share. Older cats have special qualities, like wisdom—which is only learned by living."

The kittens nervously walked in the front door of the Home for Aged Cats. Much to their surprise, jumping into a lap brought them great joy. Many of the older cats knitted scarves and mittens. They found it amusing when the kittens played with the large balls of yarn. The kittens chased pieces of paper and batted drinking straws that had fallen to the floor. Some of the older cats invented games for the kittens to play, and many of them joined in the games with the kittens.

When the kittens were exhausted, they discovered that something as simple as lying next to someone in bed brought them pleasure. During this quiet time, the kittens and the older cats shared stories. The older cats related tales of things that had happened when they were kittens. When the kittens asked questions, the older cats were very patient and understanding. The kittens found that reassuring.

The older cats had such a good time that the young kittens were invited to visit weekly. Each week, the day they visited was called "Kitten Day," and each week, the older cats greeted them with warm smiles. Now the kittens realized that what Pushpa said was true: "You each can make a positive contribution in this world." By their simple act of kindness, the kittens were rewarded by feeling needed, valued, and important.

> Pushpa's **energy and enthusiasm inspire** other kittens to do good things.

ACTIVITIES

Questions to promote interaction and understanding of this Character Link:

- How did Pushpa inspire others?
- Why did the kittens respond to her suggestions?
- What did the kittens learn from Pushpa?
- How did Pushpa make tasks fun to do?
- How did the kittens benefit by participating with Pushpa?
- Why is it critical to feel needed, valued, and important?

Separate the children into three groups, as follows:

Group #1: Give this group musical instruments to play. Ask them to play with energy and enthusiasm as they march and chant:

Character Links, Character Links,

There seem to be so many!

But master one and then go on

And soon you'll master many.

Meow! Meow! Meow!

We'll teach you how!

Join us. March in our parade.

We'll learn the Links together.

Group #2: Give this group a sign that reads, "Come join our group." Tell them to sit quietly holding the sign and show no enthusiasm.

Group #3: Ask the remaining children which group they would like to join. Why do they feel that way? Which group had the most fun?

This exercise demonstrates that energy and enthusiasm are "caught," not "taught!"

Choose an area of the playroom that needs to be tidied up. Ask for several volunteers to be "role models," using energy and enthusiasm to inspire the other children to participate in the cleanup. Ask the group what qualities the children who are role models should exhibit. Make a list and discuss the qualities.

Ask to children to stand up and follow you. March around the room, laugh, make sweeping motions with your arms, make a bridge with one child and have the rest of the group pass underneath. Then make two circles, one inside the other, and have them move in opposite directions. Have the children extend their hand to each approaching child as he or she passes.

Following this activity, ask the children how they feel. Do they feel more energetic than when they were sitting and listening to the story?

11

I AM WHAT I BELIEVE

11   I AM WHAT I BELIEVE

> To *believe* means to feel strongly that something is true.

From the time Pushpa was a young kitten, she loved to paint. Getting her paws covered with paint and then making sweeping motions on the back fence brought her great joy. Pushpa's mother encouraged her. Pushpa also had teachers who recognized her talent and encouraged her painting. The teachers helped the kitten develop her talent.

Pushpa remembered her mother saying, "*To succeed at a task, the most important thing is to believe it's possible.*" She never forgot those words of wisdom. Day after day, Pushpa focused on the challenge to become an excellent painter. At first, her pictures were very primitive and unrefined. But she practiced and practiced and practiced and kept improving.

Some people laughed when they saw Pushpa her easel, painting. It wasn't easy for a cat to be accepted as an artist. She heard repeatedly, "Cats don't paint. How ridiculous!"

Her mother told her firmly, "Pushpa, when someone talks like that, it's just an opinion. When you're young, you sometimes take opinions as the truth, but the *truth* is really what you believe in your heart." With her mother's encouragement, Pushpa never lost sight of her goal to be a successful painter. However, along her journey to become a recognized painter, she experienced criticism, ridicule, and moments of disappointment, as well as moments of great joy.

Pushpa remembered fondly the librarian who helped her believe in her goal. "Of course cats can paint," the librarian told Pushpa. "Read this book titled *Why Cats Paint*." Pushpa was ecstatic when she opened the pages. In the book she saw pictures painted by Lu Lu and Wong Wong, two cats who always painted together. One of their works, called The Wonglu Triptych, sold for $19,000 at an auction in 1993.[1] This was one of the highest prices ever paid for a work of cat art. Pushpa already knew from her own experience that cats could paint, but it was such a good feeling to know that some cats even had their work hanging in art galleries in New York and Canada.

Today, Pushpa's paintings hang in several local art galleries. Her next goal is to have her painting hanging in art galleries all over the world.

> *"If you think you can, you can.*
> *If you think you can't, you can't."*
> — Henry Ford

[1]Heather Busch and Burton Silver, *Why Cats Paint*, Ten Speed Press, Berkeley, California, p. 39.

> Pushpa grew up to be a painter because she always **believed** that she could be a painter.

ACTIVITIES

Questions to promote interaction and understanding of this Character Link:

- What did Pushpa always want to be?
- What did Pushpa's mother say about succeeding at a task?
- What did Pushpa keep doing to improve her skill?
- When did Pushpa start believing that she could be successful?
- What is an opinion?
- What is the truth?
- How did Pushpa feel when she was given encouragement?
- How did Pushpa feel when she was criticized?
- What goals did Pushpa set?
- What does the quote from Henry Ford mean to you?

    "If you think you can, you can.
    If you think you can't, you can't."

Form a circle and repeat:

Character Links, Character Links,

There seem to be so many!

But master one and then go on

And soon you'll master many.

Why is it important to have people support you? Name someone who supports you. How does this person help you to learn and grow? What are some things you would like to do, but that you need support to accomplish?

In the circle, have each child ask for support in trying to do one specific thing: "I need support when I am trying to _____!"

The other children repeat: "We know you can _____. We promise to support your efforts."

Why is setting goals important? What is one goal that you would like to accomplish? How hard would you be willing to work to accomplish it? What is the first step to take toward achieving your goal?

12

I CHOOSE MY OWN THOUGHTS

12 I CHOOSE MY OWN THOUGHTS

To *choose* means to pick between two or more things.
Thoughts are the ideas you have in your mind.

Chadwick was a cat who enjoyed thinking. He had heard about the power of thoughts. He remembered hearing other cats say, "What you think about is what you get!" When he asked what that meant, they replied, "This simply means that if you think negative thoughts, bad things seem to happen to you. If you think positive thoughts, good things seem to happen more often."

Recently Chadwick was having a lot of bad dreams at night. Some were so terrifying that he called them nightmares. In one recurring nightmare, a large monster appeared and started chasing him. He ran as fast as his little legs would carry him. As fast as he ran, he was never able to outrun the monster. He escaped only when he woke up. When he awakened, Chadwick was trembling and terrified, and also sure that the monster must be in his bedroom.

When he called out for help, his mother and father came right away. After checking everywhere, they assured Chadwick that there was no monster in his room—it was just in his thoughts. He knew that his mother and father loved him very much, and because he trusted them, it helped a lot. However, the monster kept coming back in his dreams.

Chadwick decided to talk to his parents about thoughts, sharing that he had heard that thoughts were powerful. They agreed that thoughts were very powerful. Then they asked him, "How do you think you could use thoughts to help solve your problem?"

Chadwick thought about positive, happy thoughts, and he thought about negative, unhappy thoughts. Then he had an idea. "I can choose my own thoughts. What if I thought a really good thought, just before closing my eyes and going to sleep?"

His parents said, "Great idea! Why don't you give it a try?"

That night, as Chadwick was being tucked in bed, his mother asked him, "What good thought are you going to think tonight?"

Chadwick paused before answering, "I'll dream of Grandma." Chadwick's grandmother loved him very much and Chadwick knew it. He loved the stories she read to him and the games they played together.

He awakened the next morning feeling rested—no nightmares at all. He shared this with his mother and father. He asked, "If some night the monster comes back, will you help me? I would like you to help me sweep him out of my room."

His mother replied, "Of course. It's always wise to have a plan in case that ever happens again. However, if you remember to think good thoughts at bedtime, that monster may never come back."

> Chadwick **chooses the thoughts** in his head before going to sleep at night.

ACTIVITIES

Questions to promote interaction and understanding of this Character Link:

- How did Chadwick learn that thoughts were powerful?
- When did he learn that he could choose his own thoughts?
- When did he ask for help from his parents?
- What did his parents do to help Chadwick?
- Why was it important for Chadwick to work on choosing good thoughts?
- How did it work when Chadwick chose a nice thought before falling asleep?
- How did that affect Chadwick's belief about thoughts?
- When do you think that Chadwick will remember again that he can choose his thoughts?

In the illustration, what does the dark cloud represent? What are some negative thoughts?

In the illustration, what does the sun represent? What are some positive thoughts?

As you listen to the following story, see if you can tell who has positive thoughts and who has negative thoughts.

The sun was shining when Chadwick went to invite his friend out to play. His friend came to the door, looked at the sky, and said, "I see a dark cloud. It's going to rain."

Chadwick responded, "But the sun is shining and it isn't raining now."

"That's true," said his friend, "but I know that it's going to rain and I don't like getting my fur wet." With that, his friend closed the door, leaving Chadwick to play by himself.

- Who had negative thoughts about the weather?
- Who had positive thoughts about the weather?
- Who enjoyed the sunshine?
- Who has the most fun and happiness in life?
- Who misses a lot of life?

What thoughts can you think of that will allow you to enjoy the moment and have many wonderful experiences?

What negative thoughts can you think of that might limit the good times in your life?

What steps can you take to help you choose positive thoughts?

Thoughts can be changed! Pretend that you have a clicker in your hand, and by pressing the finger of one hand into the palm of the other hand, you can change the picture in your mind.

Everyone picture a scary monster in your mind. Now, use your finger-clicker. Press your finger into your palm and change the picture to something pleasant that makes you feel good.

Ask each child, "What was your good picture?"

13

I USE MY IMAGINATION DAILY

13   I USE MY IMAGINATION DAILY

> *Imagination* is the ability to see a picture, feel a sensation,
> hear a sound, or taste or smell something in your mind.

One day Misifu said to her mother, "I'm bored. I don't know what to do."

"You can do anything or be anything you want," her mother replied. "Just use your imagination."

Misifu looked at her mother and said, "I don't think that I understand what imagination is all about."

"Would you like to try something that might make imagination much clearer?" Misifu's mother asked. The little cat nodded.

Misifu's mother asked her to find a comfortable spot and close her eyes. Then she said, "I will describe something to you. Listen to what I describe, and see if you can picture it in your mind. When I ring this bell, I want you to let go of that picture. Then I will describe something new to you." She began:

A horse galloping across a grassy meadow, his mane and tail flying in the wind. (In a few seconds, she rang the bell.)

A sailboat moving swiftly through the water, its purple and orange sail billowing in the wind. (Again, she rang the bell.)

Waves crashing upon a rocky shore. (She rang the bell.)

Biting into a sour lemon. (Misifu was glad when she heard the bell!)

Licking pink, sweet frosting from a mixing bowl. (It tasted so good, Misifu didn't want her mother to ring the bell.)

Smelling a beautiful bouquet of fragrant pink roses.

Finally, she asked Misifu to open her eyes. "Were you able to see the galloping horse? The sailboat moving through the water with its purple and orange sail? The waves crashing on the shore? Could you imagine biting into a sour lemon, licking pink frosting from a mixing bowl, and smelling the bouquet of roses?"

Misifu said, "Yes, it all seemed so real!" Her imagination allowed her to form pictures of things that weren't really there.

Her mother continued, "Imagination also lets you see yourself doing things successfully—even things that you don't yet know how to do."

Now Misifu realized that she *did* use her imagination. She just didn't realize that was the word for it. Every day she played make-believe. Sometimes she was a fire-cat, putting out fires and saving little kittens from the burning flames. Other times she was an astro-cat, traveling in a spacecraft to the moon. Misifu also imagined herself writing books, printing each of the words correctly. And she imagined herself sitting in a sunny corner, reading her books to her friends—even though she wasn't quite able to read yet.

She also imagined herself in her own kitchen, baking delicious cookies all by herself.

Misifu's imagination allowed her to see all the different things she could become. However, she knew that it would take more than imagination to become what she saw in her mind. She knew her imagination had to be combined with hard work and perseverance. For example, Misifu realized that she would never bake cookies all by herself if she didn't learn how, and practice. She practiced making cookies with her mother's help every available opportunity. One day, she would be able to bake cookies without her mother's assistance, but *only* if she made them over and over until she learned how. Still, the first step was imagining that she could do it.

Misifu's mother believed imagination was so important that she told Misifu about Albert Einstein. He was a famous scientist and mathematician who said:

"Imagination is more important than knowledge."

Misifu uses her **imagination** daily when she plays make-believe.

ACTIVITIES

Questions to promote interaction and understanding of this Character Link:

- When Misifu closed her eyes and saw pictures in her mind, what skill was she using?
- When you close your eyes and imagine biting a lemon, what happens?
- When you think of licking your favorite ice cream cone, what happens in your mouth?
- When you "make believe" that you're inside a magical castle, what are you using?
- When you daydream, what are you doing?
- How valuable is it to be able to see something in your mind?
- What can you do to change the picture in your mind?
- How does the picture in your mind affect your future?
- What do you need besides imagination to make the picture come true?
- Why do you think that the quote by Albert Einstein is important?
- What does that quote mean to you?

Play a game of "What you can see, you can be." Encourage all the children to use their imagination to see what may be in their future. Encourage their imaginations by asking questions:

- What would you like to be when you are grown?
- What do you enjoy doing today that you could use in the future?
- How do you see yourself using this talent?

Share stories of your favorite public figures who have had successful careers. Share with them the obstacles many successful people have had to overcome to realize the fulfillment of their dreams—dreams first created in their imagination.

Go outside on a beautiful day when there are puffy clouds in the sky. Lie on mats or blankets and describe what shapes the clouds suggest. Share and affirm what the children see.

14

I HAVE EMPATHY

14 I HAVE EMPATHY

> Having *empathy* means identifying with and understanding another person's situation, feelings, and motives.

Moo-Moo was lying in her own driveway, observing. Cats love to sit and observe. She was fascinated by two kittens playing tackle. They would look at each other, heads down, tails swaying back and forth, and then suddenly pounce. Once entangled, they playfully rolled in the grass, making pretend bites on tails and legs, backs and tummies. They would then separate and the dance would begin all over again. It was delightful to watch and very entertaining.

Moo-Moo suddenly heard a terrifying racket. Before she could move, she was hit by an "out of control" skateboarder. She felt a terrible pain in her right leg and let out a loud, painful MEOW.

Heather ran to the driveway. She could see that something was terribly wrong with Moo-Moo's leg. Heather carefully helped her cat into the car and drove straight to the veterinarian. X-rays showed that the leg was broken. The veterinarian set the bone and put on a cast. Moo-Moo couldn't put any weight on the broken leg, so she was given crutches and sent home with Heather to rest and heal.

Friends heard about her accident, and they brought her flowers and treats.

Chadwick rushed over when he heard. He had great empathy for Moo-Moo. He had never broken a leg, but he could imagine how uncomfortable and hot it must be to have a cast on your leg. He could also imagine how he would feel if he couldn't run and play outside. He brought a big mound of fresh catnip and her favorite flower, a gardenia. Moo-Moo loved the perfume of the gardenia.

Chadwick offered to bring his wagon to pull Moo-Moo to school. "There's enough walking to do after you get there," Chadwick said. Moo-Moo was grateful and accepted his kind offer. He pulled her to and from school every day. When she walked with her crutches, Chadwick walked slowly with her.

She couldn't wait for the cast to come off and to be her old self again. Until the cast was off, Moo-Moo was grateful for the love, concern, and empathy expressed by all of her friends.

> Chadwick has **empathy** for Moo-Moo when he understands
> how it feels to be on crutches, unable to run and play.

ACTIVITIES

Questions to promote interaction and understanding of this Character Link:

- What does it mean to have empathy?
- Why do you have to use your imagination before you can express empathy?
- When did Chadwick use his imagination to understand Moo-Moo's situation?
- How did Chadwick's imagination help him express empathy for Moo-Moo?
- What helped Moo-Moo the most after her accident?
- How will Moo-Moo's accident increase her ability to express empathy for kittens in similar circumstances?
- When someone is hurting physically or hurting emotionally, what is most appreciated?
- Why is it important to be able to express empathy?

Empathy means the ability to understand another's situation. Take a piece of acrylic plastic and smear Vaseline® on one-half of the plastic. Pass the plastic around the circle and ask the children to look through the side that is smeared. Hold up a card with a picture containing fine details. Then ask them to look through the clean side of the plastic at the same picture. Discuss the experience.

- How did you feel while looking through the smeared side of the plastic?
- How did you feel looking through the clear side?

- What do you think was the point of the exercise?
- How would you feel if you had to look through the blurred side of the plastic all day?
- How do you feel about children who are look through the blurred side of the plastic all day long, unless they wear glasses to make the picture clear?
- How does this exercise help you to express empathy?

How would you feel if you had hurt feelings, and when you expressed those hurt feelings, everyone ignored you?

What can you do to develop your ability to express empathy? For example:

- Be aware of other children's situations.
- Use your imagination to put yourself in another child's situation.
- Be a better listener.
- Use your imagination to picture yourself expressing empathy.

15

I APPRECIATE EVERY DAY

15   I APPRECIATE EVERY DAY

> To *appreciate* means to understand the value
> of something and to be thankful for it.

John Louie sat basking in the sunshine. The warmth made him feel very warm and cozy. He thought of all the things he appreciated every single day.

Air to breathe
And sunshine to bask in.
Comfortable pink cushions to lie on.
Clear, cold water to drink
And dip your paws in.
Games to play and bugs to observe.
The shade of a tree on a hot summer day.
Grass to lie on
And clouds to watch.
Gentle breezes to tickle your whiskers.
Flowers to smell and catnip to chew,
Pepe and Chadwick and Moo-Moo, too.
Liang and Yulan and Lettuce the turtle.
Pushpa and Heather
And friends Chipie, Hedgie, and Birdie.
Fathers and mothers
Sisters and brothers
Aunts and uncles
Cousins and others.

Loving homes filled with caring people.
Smiles and hugs and loving embraces.
Kind words and soft voices
From joyous, uplifting people.
Encouragement given by parents and teachers.
Peace and quiet, alone time to dream.
Moments to share and moments to care
And show one's compassion.
And for just being alive
John Louie gave his utmost appreciation.

> John Louie **appreciates** the warmth of the sunshine every day.

ACTIVITIES

Questions to promote interaction and understanding of this Character Link:

- What are some of the things that John Louie appreciated?
- How expensive were the things he appreciated?
- Who are some of the people that John Louie appreciated?
- Why did John Louie feel that it was important to express appreciation every day?

Ask the children to stop for a few minutes, close their eyes, and think silently about things that they are grateful for.

Have the children name aloud one thing that they are grateful for today.

What do you take for granted every day that many children in the world don't have? (For example, parents, food, shelter, shoes, clothing.)

When you want something and it doesn't happen, how do you feel? How does this change your feelings about being grateful?

When you feel that you are lacking something like a toy or a game, what happens to your feelings of appreciation?

Go outside and have the children look for things to enjoy and appreciate. Some suggestions might include flowers, trees, birds, insects, plants, animals, clouds, sunshine, classmates to play with and share conversation, playground equipment, and kind supervision.

Ask the children how it feels after they have expressed their appreciation.

16

I ENJOY SHARING WITH OTHERS

16 I ENJOY SHARING WITH OTHERS

> To *share* means to have or use something together with others, and to take turns. It can also mean to divide something into parts to give to others. You can share your toys; you can share food; you can also share a smile or a friendly greeting.

Chadwick's mother packed a very tasty lunch for him to take to school. He had a catfish sandwich with his favorite mayonnaise and two catnip cookies.

Liang sat beside him at lunchtime. Chadwick asked, "Where's your lunch?"

"I forgot it," replied Liang.

"I'm hungry," Chadwick said. "Are you hungry too?"

Liang answered, "Yes, I am."

Chadwick looked at his favorite sandwich and his two cookies. He really wanted to eat it all. Silent for a moment, Chadwick then asked, "Would you like half of my catfish sandwich?"

Liang smiled. "I'd love part of your catfish sandwich. Catfish sandwiches are my favorite. Are you sure that you want to share?"

"Yes and no," said Chadwick. "I could eat the whole sandwich, but I know how I'd feel if I had forgotten my lunch. I would want someone to share their lunch with me."

Chadwick reached into his lunch box and offered half of his sandwich. Liang thanked him, and they both savored the taste of the catfish. He offered Liang one of his catnip cookies.

"Are you sure?" Liang asked.

"I'm sure," answered Chadwick. After eating the cookies, Liang thanked him again for sharing.

Chadwick said, "Sharing my lunch with you felt good."

Liang said that it made her feel really good too. Liang admitted that she found sharing very difficult at times. She had a younger brother who always wanted to play with her toys, and at times it was very annoying. She shared some toys, but others were very precious to her, and these she was not willing to share. Chadwick said he felt the same way. There were some things that he wasn't willing to share with anyone.

Liang said, "My mother always reminds me that there are lots of things to share besides toys. You can share a part of you, like a smile or a friendly greeting. You can share feelings and stories and love and hugs. Sharing includes so many things that we all can afford to share. Sharing makes others feel better, but the biggest reward goes to the one who shares."

> Chadwick **enjoyed sharing** his sandwich with Liang.

ACTIVITIES

Questions to promote interaction and understanding of this Character Link:

- When Liang asked if Chadwick really wanted to share, and he said, "Yes and no," what Character Link was Chadwick practicing? (I am honest.)
- Chadwick said, "I could eat the whole sandwich, but I know how I'd feel if I had forgotten my sandwich." What Character Link was he demonstrating here? (I have empathy.)
- How do you feel about Liang's statement that there are some things that she is not willing to share?
- Why did Chadwick "feel good" after sharing his lunch with Liang?
- How do you feel about sharing a smile and a friendly greeting?
- What is the cost of sharing hugs and love?
- How do you feel when you make someone feel better as a result of your behavior?

Good manners are one way to make someone feel better. When someone says "please" and "thank you" to you, how do you feel?

When you are in a new situation and someone greets you in a warm and friendly manner, how does that make you feel?

When you are asked to take turns, what are your feelings?

When your mother bakes cookies for you and your friends after school, how does that make you feel?

When someone is willing to sit and read a story to you, how does that make you feel?

When someone includes you in activities, they are sharing time and themselves with you. How do you feel about expressing appreciation for their efforts?

Let's share a time when someone did something for you that was very nice. For example, here are some nice things people might do for you:

- Planning a birthday party.
- Going with you on a school field trip.
- Taking you to the library.
- Taking you to a children's museum.
- Reading stories to you.
- Helping you to learn how to make a salad.
- Helping you learn how to make delicious cookies.
- Taking you to swimming lessons.
- Playing your favorite game with you.
- Taking you to your favorite restaurant.
- Helping you to pick out a Halloween costume.
- Making a favorite Halloween costume for you.
- Taking you to see a movie.
- Taking you to the park to play on the swings.

How many of you have taken a moment to thank people who have shared their time with you?

Let's all say together:
Character Links, Character Links,
There seem to be so many!
But master one and then move on
And soon you'll master many.

17

I AM PATIENT

17 I AM PATIENT

Being *patient* means putting up with delay, or waiting, without becoming angry or upset.

Moo-Moo sat by the oven door, breathing in the wonderful smells of the baking catnip cookies. She had been watching the cookies for just a few minutes, but it seemed like a very long time. She licked her lips in anticipation.

Heather said, "The time will pass quickly if you help me clean the mixing bowl, measuring spoons, and cups. I would really appreciate your help. You can still smell the cookies while you're helping me. I promise you'll have the very first cookie when they're done."

As Heather washed the dishes, Moo-Moo dried them and put them away. "Learning to be patient isn't easy," Heather said. "It's important to remember that impatience can cause serious problems. Yesterday, when we were in the car, remember the driver who went through the red light, narrowly missing the car in front of us?" Moo-Moo did remember. It was very frightening and made her shiver when she thought what might have happened to the people in the car.

"Being patient is a sign of growing up and assuming responsibility," Heather said. Moo-Moo remembered John Louie's experience when he didn't look both ways before crossing the street and was almost hit by a car. He had been impatient, and it nearly cost him his life.

The oven buzzer sounded. Heather removed the cookie sheet from the oven. When the cookies cooled, Heather offered the first cookie to Moo-Moo. Yummy, it tasted so good!

There was a time, not long ago, when Moo-Moo could hardly wait for the ingredients to be combined in the mixing bowl before eating the raw cookie dough. It tasted good, but nothing like a freshly baked cookie. She was learning to be patient. Now she could wait for them to bake. Like many of the Character Links, learning to be patient took work and wasn't easy. She remembered the poem:

Character Links, Character Links,
There seem to be so many!
But master one and then go on
And soon you'll master many.

> Moo-Moo is **patient** while waiting for the cookies to bake.

ACTIVITIES

Questions to promote interaction and understanding of this Character Link:

- Sometimes time seems to pass quickly, and other times slowly. How did the time pass when Moo-Moo was sitting on the stool watching the cookies baking?
- What did Heather suggest that would make the time seem to pass more quickly?
- When Moo-Moo was busy actively doing something with Heather, how did the time pass?
- How do you think Moo-Moo felt while she was helping Heather?
- What feeling or Character Link was Moo-Moo experiencing? (I am needed, valued, and important.)
- What almost happened to John Louie when he was impatient, or not patient?
- What almost happened when the car went through the red light?
- How was the driver acting? (The driver was not acting responsibly and he was impatient.)
- What did Moo-Moo do with the cookie dough before she started developing patience?
- What tasted better to Moo-Moo?

What are some situations in which it is difficult for you to be patient? What are some things you could do that would help you to develop patience?

When you are learning a new task, why is it important to learn to be patient with yourself?

What are some of the rewards for being patient?

An activity that demonstrates the rewards of being patient is planting seeds.

Have several small trays filled with dirt. Allow each child to plant a row of seeds.

Each day have the children place the seeds in the sun.

Each day have the children water the seeds.

It requires patience to wait for the green leaves to push through the dirt.

What is the reward after caring for the seeds? What would happen if you dug up the seed every day to see what's happening?

We can draw a parallel between a child's growth and the seed's growth. Just as the seed grows slowly and requires patience for change to occur, learning the Character Links requires patience, because it takes time for you to grow and for changes to take place in you. Slowly you will become more patient in all areas of your life.

Remember:

Character Links, Character Links,
There seem to be so many!
But master one and then go on
And soon you'll master many.

18

I AM UNIQUE

18   I AM UNIQUE

> Being *unique* means there is no one exactly like you.

Yulan was unique. She was a Selkirk, a breed of cat with curly fur and curly whiskers. Some cats have long fur and some have short fur, but either way, most cats have fur that is perfectly straight. Not Yulan. She looked like she had been crimped with a miniature curling iron. Her curly fur was soft and silky. Everyone wanted to pick her up and cuddle her. She was as plush and huggable as a toy animal. She enjoyed this.

The part Yulan did *not* like was being teased by other kittens because she was different. Then when she was four months old, her curls disappeared and she looked like other kittens. The teasing stopped. Yulan was so relieved, until her mother said, "Come sit on my lap. There's something we need to talk about. It's normal for Selkirks to lose their curls at four months. It's also normal for a Selkirk's coat to start curling again at eight months. In fact, the curls will get curlier until you are two years old." Yulan sighed. The teasing wasn't over.

Her mother heard Yulan's heavy sigh and asked gently, "How do you feel about the way my fur looks?"

Yulan replied, "You're the most beautiful cat in the whole world."

"Well, you're going to look just like me when you grow up."

Yulan smiled. She understood the point her mother was making.

Her mother continued, "Every cat has qualities that make that cat unique. It's important to remember that even though every cat is unique, all cats are also the same inside."

Yulan looked confused. Her mother gave examples to help her understand. "All cats—whether they are chubby or slender, whether they have stripes, patterns, or spots; long fur or short; curly or straight fur; green, blue, or gold eyes—no matter what they look like outside, they all have similar feelings inside. Everyone hurts. Everyone needs to be loved and hugged, wanted, accepted, and valued." Yulan was beginning to understand.

Then her mother said, "You have to find out who you are. Accepting who you are and just being who you are is one of the most difficult tasks in life. You're very sensitive because of what's happened to you. What a wonderful mother you will be to your own kittens, because you have experienced what it's like to be different. Think what a wonderful cat counselor you could be. Yulan, *celebrate your uniqueness!*"

Her mother had given Yulan much to think about.

> Yulan is **unique** because of her personal characteristics and curly fur.

ACTIVITIES

Questions to promote interaction and understanding of this Character Link:

- Why was Yulan unique in appearance?
- What did Yulan enjoy about her appearance?
- What happened to Yulan that she didn't like?
- How did she feel when her curls started disappearing?
- How did she feel upon learning from her mother that her curls would come back?
- What makes every single cat unique?
- What makes you unique?
- How can every cat be unique, but at the same time be the same as every other cat?
- What feelings does every cat share with every other cat in the world?
- Why does Yulan's mother say, "Accepting who you are is one of the most difficult tasks in life"?
- What does "Celebrate your uniqueness" mean?

Form a circle and have the children describe the unique qualities of their families. This could include the number of members in the family; what they like to do together; their pets and the pets' names; where they go on vacations; their favorite foods and activities.

Have a chart with each child's name listed. Select one child to be in the center of the circle. Go around the circle, having the children in turn name a quality that they like about the child in the center of the circle. For example, they might mention that the child is enthusiastic, caring, willing to share, fun to play with, honest, respectful or responsible, willing to help others, or that the child smiles a lot, says nice things to others, and so forth.

Make a list of all the feelings common to everyone. Follow the suggestions of the children. For example:

We can feel . . .

joy	gratitude	hostility
fear	anger	love
happiness	frustration	sadness
resentment	appreciation	affection
pain	pleasure	excitement

We can also feel . . .

peaceful	energetic	curious
depressed	bored	lonely
rejected	stimulated	comfortable
tired	unappreciated	sulking
uncomfortable	embarrassed	generous

Have the children practice making feeling faces and ask the other children to guess the emotion they are expressing.

Distribute paper and crayons and ask the children to draw an emotion that they experienced today. Make masks of these emotions by cutting out their drawings. This emotion is unique to them. It is to be respected and listened to carefully.

19

I AM CURIOUS

19   I AM CURIOUS

> Being *curious* means being eager to learn about things
> that are new, strange, or interesting.

John Louie was a curious cat. He was always wondering, "Why? Why does it get dark? Why does the sun come up?" He was equally curious about bags and boxes that came in the house. He always wondered, "What's inside?"

Heather carried in a bag of groceries and set the bag on the floor. Immediately, John Louie wondered, "What's inside?" When he stood on his hind feet looking into the bag, it tipped over. Then, he crawled into the bag looking for anchovy popcorn, his favorite treat. There was nothing but fruits and vegetables. John Louie backed out of the bag, feeling disappointed.

Heather started unpacking the bag of groceries. Noticing the look of disappointment on John Louie's face, she said "I'm going to fix something special for you. I think you'll like it."

John Louie couldn't imagine what that might be. Heather held up an ear of corn. "John Louie, do you know where popcorn comes from?"

John Louie said, "No." He *did* know where anchovies came from—the ocean. However, that was not the question Heather had asked him. His curiosity made him ask, "Where does popcorn come from?"

"Popcorn is made from corn," replied Heather. "I know that you think you don't like vegetables, John Louie, but you might like to try some fresh corn."

John Louie wasn't too sure about this. After all, corn was a vegetable and he did *not* like vegetables.

Heather placed the ear of corn in a pot of boiling water. In a few minutes the aroma of the cooking corn was pleasant to his sensitive nose. After the corn cooled, Heather removed the yellow kernels, placing them in John Louie's favorite blue dish. He approached carefully, sniffing the corn. Overcome by curiosity, he nibbled a small piece. What a surprise! It was delicious!

After finishing his treat, John Louie found a patch of sunlight and began washing his face. In no time he was very warm.

Other cats sat in the sun for hours on end and didn't seem to get hot. For example, his friend Pushpa never got as hot as John Louie did in the sun. His curiosity was aroused again. He asked Heather, "Why is that? Why do I get hotter than the other cats?"

Heather said, "John Louie, you have a black coat, and black absorbs (soaks up) the sunrays. Pushpa's white coat reflects (turns or throws back) the rays. Therefore, she doesn't get as warm as you do."

John Louie crawled into the empty grocery bag for shade from the hot sun. Because of Heather's help, combined with his curiosity, he'd found a delicious new treat. He had also learned two new words—*absorb* and *reflect*. He smiled as he fell asleep, wondering where his curiosity would take him tomorrow. Curiosity was a wonderful thing!

> John Louie was **curious** when he crawled into the grocery bag.

ACTIVITIES

Questions to promote interaction and understanding of this Character Link:

- What makes you think that John Louie was a curious cat?
- What was John Louie looking for when he crawled into the paper bag?
- Was Heather surprised by his behavior?
- How did John Louie feel after tipping over the bag and crawling inside?
- What did John Louie think about vegetables?
- What did John Louie think of Heather's suggestion that he might like the vegetable, corn?
- How did John Louie like the aroma of the cooking corn?
- What made him taste the freshly cooked corn?
- When he asked questions, what happened?
- Why is curiosity so important?
- Why do you think that curiosity might at times get you in trouble?
- Where do you think John Louie's curiosity will take him tomorrow?

Ask the children to name things that they are curious about. What are the ways to satisfy their curiosity? Make a list of the possible means to get answers.

What role does curiosity play in increasing our vocabulary and our understanding of words? When you hear a word that is not familiar, what can you do?

What role did curiosity play in the invention of...

- the wheel?
- the light bulb?
- the telephone?
- television?
- new drugs to fight disease?
- in-line skates?
- skateboards?

Invite the children to name some times when their curiosity got them into difficulty. Why do they believe that this happened? How can they use this information in the future?

20

I AM CARING

20   I AM CARING

> Being *caring* means having an interest, liking, or concern about a person or thing. It also means helping someone when they need it.

Yulan was a kitten who had soft, thick, curly fur. Liang often looked at Yulan jealously, wishing that she had such curly soft fur. Because Yulan looked different from the straight-haired cats, many classmates teased her about her curly coat. It was clear that the teasing hurt Yulan's feelings.

Liang had empathy for Yulan. Using her imagination, she felt she had some idea of how Yulan must feel when she was teased. However, Liang said to herself, "Feeling empathy without taking action won't help Yulan's hurt feelings." Liang wanted to do something to show Yulan she cared.

At school, Liang started smiling and talking with Yulan. At snack time she sat next to her. Liang whispered to Yulan, "I wish I had soft, curly fur like you."

Yulan said, "You don't really mean that, do you?"

Liang continued, "Yes, I really do. I think that you are beautiful."

When it was Yulan's turn to clean up after snack time, Liang volunteered to help. When someone started to tease her, Liang said, "STOP! That isn't polite." Saying STOP to the other kittens took a great deal of courage.

Liang started inviting Yulan to her home after school. Yulan seemed ill at ease when she first arrived, but Liang's mother had baked delicious catnip cookies. After sharing a saucer of warm milk and several catnip cookies, Yulan began to enjoy herself.

Both kittens loved to dress up. Liang had a pink trunk full of costumes—boas, hats, jewelry, crowns, capes, magic wands, purses, and silver and gold slippers. Soon they were both dressed up, pretending to be elegantly dressed belles of the ball. What fun they had together! Yulan wore a string of Liang's pink crystal beads around her neck that looked stunning.

As days passed, they continued to spend more time together. At school, the teasing about Yulan's curly fur stopped. Liang was grateful that defending Yulan had contributed to a change in the other kittens' behavior. It proved that one kitten can make a difference. Caring meant doing something for someone, not just thinking about it.

One afternoon Liang walked across the back fence on her way to Yulan's house. It was Yulan's birthday. Many kittens had been invited, and all had accepted the invitation to her party. Liang wore the beautiful pink crystal necklace that had looked so lovely on Yulan. When Yulan greeted her friend at the door,

Liang took the pink crystal beads from around her neck and placed them on Yulan, saying "Happy Birthday!"

A tear rolled down Yulan's cheek and off the end of her curly whisker. She said, "Thank you, Liang."

> Liang is **caring** when she invites Yulan to play at her house.

ACTIVITIES

Questions to promote interaction and understanding of this Character Link:

- If you want to be caring, why is it important to have imagination?
- Why is it important to have empathy?
- How did Liang show that she was caring?
- How did Liang show courage?
- What influence did Liang have over the behavior of the other kittens?
- When Liang said, "Feeling empathy without taking action won't help Yulan's hurt feelings," what did she mean?
- What does this statement mean: "Caring meant doing something for someone, not just thinking about it."
- What gift did Liang give Yulan for her birthday?
- What Character Link did Liang use to think of this gift?
- Why was Yulan moved to tears when she received this gift?

Caring is exhibited in many ways. What qualities are exhibited by the following?

- A crossing guard, who volunteers 45 minutes of his time every day to ensure the safety of children on their way to school.
- A parent who volunteers to go on a school field trip and drives children in her car.
- A stranger who helps a vision-impaired person cross the street safely.
- A stranger who finds a lost pet and attempts to return the pet to its owner.
- An individual who volunteers time to help a child who is having difficulty reading.
- An individual who contributes money to a disaster relief fund.
- An individual who financially supports a children's fund.
- Someone who makes the effort to meet and greet a new family moving into their neighborhood.

Invite a representative of the Red Cross to visit the class and explain what that organization does to care for people.

Ask the children to complete the sentence: "Once I helped someone by _____."

Make an opportunity for each child to contribute something to be given to a child in need during the holiday season. This could be a toy that they already own (in good condition), or a new toy.

When a child is home sick, invite the class to make a card to send to the sick child.

21

I AM ACTIVELY INVOLVED IN LIFE

21   I AM ACTIVELY INVOLVED IN LIFE

> To be *involved* means to have a necessary part in something that is happening. To be *actively involved* means to be doing your part with enthusiasm and interest.

Pepe the mouse always felt important when he could be helpful. It was difficult to lift the heavy glass jelly jar up to Chadwick. However, it had been a challenge and he had succeeded. Pepe felt good about his contribution to the sandwich making.

He hoped that one day the manufacturers would put jelly in plastic jars, like peanut butter. Then if you dropped the jar, it wouldn't be such a disaster. In fact, after lunch, he would ask Chadwick's mother to help him write a letter to the jelly company, making the suggestion about plastic and telling them why it was important. Pepe found that if he just kept wishing and hoping about things, nothing happened. However, when he actively took steps to change something, there was a good chance that it would happen.

This whole sandwich-making project resulted from a previous experience. He and Chadwick had been playing, and it was past their usual lunchtime. Suddenly hungry, they went to Chadwick's mother to ask, "When are you going to fix our lunch?"

She smiled and replied, "I know it's late, but I am very busy. Would you like to learn how to make lunch yourselves?"

Chadwick and Pepe looked at each other, then responded, "We'd rather have you make lunch for us."

Chadwick's mother suggested, "Let's discuss the advantages of learning how to make lunch for yourselves."

"Well, we could eat lunch whenever we were hungry," suggested Chadwick.

"You would learn a new skill and be moving toward independence," his mother stated. "It may seem easier not to take responsibility and to remain dependent on someone to meet your needs. However, I would really appreciate your help when I am busy."

Chadwick and Pepe had a short discussion. They decided to learn how to make sandwiches for themselves.

In the beginning, they needed much guidance. At first, they spread the peanut butter too hard and the bread fell apart. Sometimes, they didn't spread the peanut butter all the way to the edge, resulting in dry mouthfuls of bread. Sometimes they forgot the jelly, and the peanut butter stuck to the roof of their mouths. However, with practice, they became capable sandwich makers.

Today they sat at the table and ate their sandwiches. Chadwick and Pepe both felt good about their new skill and their independence. Being involved had made them feel capable. Having mastered this task, they were eager to become involved in another project.

> Pepe is **actively involved** in making lunch when he hands the jelly jar to Chadwick.

ACTIVITIES

Questions to promote interaction and understanding of this Character Link:

- How did Pepe feel when he was helpful?
- How did Pepe feel about sitting around "hoping and wishing" for something to be different?
- What did Pepe find frequently happened when he got actively involved?
- How did Chadwick and Pepe feel about being dependent on Chadwick's mother to prepare lunch?
- Why did they like things the way they were?
- How did they feel about being responsible when Chadwick's mother first asked them if they would like to learn how to make their own lunch?
- When they gave the lunch subject some thought, how did they feel about learning?
- How difficult was it to learn how to make sandwiches?
- How did they feel about their independence?

In the following sentences, who is actively involved in life and who is not?

- John Louie spends the afternoon watching television.
- Pushpa helps her mother wash the dishes when they are baking cookies.
- Chadwick and Pepe want someone to make them sandwiches.
- Chadwick discovers that when you mix yellow and blue paint you make a new color—green.
- Pushpa stops playing because her feelings are hurt.
- John Louie falls asleep at his desk in school.
- Pushpa pulls weeds in the community garden.
- When the teacher asks for help, Moo-Moo volunteers.
- Chadwick pulls Moo-Moo to school in his red wagon.
- Liang invites Yulan to play at her home.
- Pushpa visits the Home for Aged Cats.
- Chadwick listens to his grandmother read a story.
- Moo-Moo keeps walking until she finds shelter.
- Misifu uses her imagination daily.

Invite the children to take turns giving examples of how they are actively involved in life.

Invite the children to suggest an area in which they would like to become actively involved. Assist the children in deciding what the first steps should be to get involved in the area of their choice.

22

I ENJOY WORKING WITH OTHERS

22 I ENJOY WORKING WITH OTHERS

To *enjoy* means to get pleasure from something. *Working* means using your energy and abilities to accomplish something. *Working with others* means being part of a team.

Moo-Moo and Misifu sat together talking. The sun was warm and the breeze was gentle. Misifu had heard that there was a sand castle contest at the beach today. They both enjoyed beach time. They liked making paw prints in the wet sand. They liked walking in the cool water as the waves washed up on the shore. Misifu said, "Let's enter the contest."

Moo-Moo said, "Why not? It would be fun, and we're both very good at digging in the sand."

On the path to the beach, they passed Hedgie the hedgehog and Chipie the chipmunk. "Come join us," said Moo-Moo. "We're entering the sand castle contest. We need your help."

Chipie and Hedgie both said, "Yes, we'd love to, but what can we do?"

Misifu replied, "You can help us decide when we get to the beach."

At the beach, the four friends held a short meeting. It was agreed that Moo-Moo and Misifu would be in charge of getting buckets of wet sand and they would build the walls of the sand castle.

Chipie would hunt for small shells and carry them back in his cheek pockets. He would press them into the walls of the castle for decoration. Hedgie would dig the moat and press his prickly back into the base of the walls to make a wonderful pattern.

They worked hard for several hours, each grateful for the contribution of the others. The buckets of wet sand were heavy. Sometimes Misifu and Moo-Moo had to help each other lift an extra-heavy bucket. They packed the sand into shapes and made the castle walls. Then they carved and molded them using their front paws. It took a lot of effort and energy.

It was a grand castle with many towers and moats. The four friends stood back admiring their project. It had been such fun, and it wouldn't have been possible if they hadn't worked together. The judges were coming as Moo-Moo placed a feather on the tallest tower of the castle.

Where do you think they placed in the contest?

> Moo-Moo and Misifu **enjoy working with** Hedgie and Chipie
> to build a sand castle.

ACTIVITIES

Questions to promote interaction and understanding of this Character Link:

- Why did Misifu and Moo-Moo decide to enter the sand castle competition?
- What did they like about the beach?
- Why did they invite Chipie and Hedgie to join them?
- How did they decide what each of them would do?
- What skills did Chipie and Hedgie have that were helpful?
- What made it possible for the group to complete their sand castle?
- Why is it important to learn to work together?
- What made the contest such fun?

What are some behaviors that make it enjoyable to work together?

How important are manners when people work together? What are some basic manners to remember? (Following are some examples.)

- Saying please and thank you.
- Saying "Excuse me."
- Saying "I'm sorry."
- Listening to suggestions of other members of your group.
- Inviting rather than ordering.
- Showing appreciation.
- Recognizing each individual's contribution.
- Showing respect for everyone.
- Sharing information that makes the project easier.
- Sharing materials.
- Taking turns.
- Being fair.
- Offering encouragement.
- Sharing the limelight if you are the leader.
- Giving deserved and specific compliments.
- Being willing to follow as well as lead.

What makes it unpleasant to work with someone who does any of these things?

- Constantly gives orders and directions.
- Acts as a director without regard for others' feelings.
- Is unfair—does not treat group members equally.
- Doesn't listen to members' suggestions.
- Gives no credit to members of the group.
- Interrupts when other people are speaking.
- Feels that he or she always has the right answers.
- Takes all the credit for the project.
- Criticizes, blames, and complains about everything.
- Uses put-downs.

What are the benefits of working together with others to accomplish a task? (Children frequently learn best when learning from each other.)

Make a list of activities that require group cooperation.

23

I AM A GOOD LISTENER

23　I AM A GOOD LISTENER

> Being a *good listener* means paying attention
> in order to hear and understand.

Liang was playing with one of Chadwick's toys. It was a very colorful rooster that cried out "Cock-a-doodle-do" when it was pulled along the floor. The faster she pulled, the more "Cock-a-doodle-doing" it did. She was running and pulling the toy around the corner when the wheel caught on a table leg. The wheel came off.

Liang felt terrible. It was Chadwick's favorite toy and she had broken it. She saw Pushpa and called out, "Oh, Pushpa! Please come and help me!" A tear rolled down Liang's cheek, and Pushpa put a paw around Liang as she sobbed out her story.

Pushpa never interrupted while Liang was speaking. She listened very carefully, nodding now and then to let Liang know that she was listening, and that she was hearing what her friend was saying.

When Liang finished, Pushpa said, "I can understand how you feel. I'd feel terrible too, if I broke something that belonged to someone else. What are your thoughts about what to do?"

Liang said, "I don't know. I suppose I have to tell Chadwick exactly what happened."

Pushpa agreed that telling Chadwick was important. Pushpa, having learned to be resourceful, also suggested, "My father is very good at fixing things. Shall we take the rooster to him and see what he says?"

Liang replied excitedly, "Yes, yes, yes!"

Pushpa's father examined the toy carefully. "There's nothing seriously broken. I have some wonderful glue that will reattach the wheel. It will make the toy as good as new." Liang gave a sigh of relief. Pushpa's father reattached the wheel, and Liang thanked him for mending the toy.

Then Liang thanked Pushpa for listening to her, and for helping her to solve the problem. She said proudly, "I'm off to return the toy to Chadwick. I'll tell him everything that happened, and remind him to let the glue dry before he starts playing with his toy again."

Liang acted responsibly when she accepted her role in breaking Chadwick's toy. She was honest when she decided to tell Chadwick. She was trustworthy when she explained the repair to Chadwick, making sure that he allowed time for the glue to dry. Pushpa smiled. She was very proud of her friend Liang.

> Pushpa is a **good listener** when she listens to Liang explaining why she is so sad.

ACTIVITIES

Questions to promote interaction and understanding of this Character Link:

- What qualities did Pushpa show that made her a good listener?
- Why is it important to not interrupt when you are listening to someone?
- Why is it important for Pushpa to show that she is listening by looking directly at Liang?
- How would Liang feel if Pushpa were looking all around the room?
- Why was it important for Pushpa to say, "I understand how you feel"?
- Why was it important for Liang to take responsibility for breaking Chadwick's toy?
- Why is it important to tell Chadwick what happened?
- Why will Chadwick think that Liang is trustworthy?
- What does being a good listener mean to you?
- Why is being a good listener important?
- When do you start learning to be a good listener?
- Where do you learn to be a good listener?
- How do you learn to be a good listener?
- What are some of the obstacles that interfere with good listening?

In the classroom have the children form a circle. The leader prints a simple sentence on a card. (Example: My cat likes three hard biscuits and two soft kitty treats.) She whispers the sentence into the ear of the first child in the circle. The leader asks that child to whisper the sentence into the next child's ear. They continue doing this until the last child in the circle hears the sentence. The leader then asks the last child to repeat out loud what she or he heard. The leader reads the sentence on the card to compare the two. This exercise demonstrates how difficult it is to listen and hear what is said.

What happens when we fail to listen? (For example: We get the directions wrong; or we misunderstand something that was said.)

Name the people in your life who are good listeners. What do they do that makes you believe they are good listeners?

Ask the children, "What can we do to improve our listening skills?" Go around the circle for suggestions. Here are some examples of important things we can do:

- Have the desire to become a better listener.
- Develop patience.
- Be interested and caring.
- Not interrupt when someone is speaking.
- Pay attention to hear and understand what is said.
- Avoid distractions.
- Make eye contact with the person speaking.
- Take responsibility for listening effectively.
- Send for tapes and movies to learn how to be a better listener.
- Go to the librarian and ask for books on listening and have someone read the information to you.
- Share the information you learn with others.
- Realize that listening is a learned skill.

Have the children share with the group their feelings about their own listening skills. Invite comments from other children. Do they agree with the child's assessment of his or her own skills? If they do, name one quality that supports this. If they disagree, they should give a specific example of why they disagree.

24

I AM A GOOD FRIEND

24 I AM A GOOD FRIEND

> A *friend* is someone you like and trust—and who
> feels the same way about you.

Misifu and John Louie sat with their paws around each other. They had been friends for a long time. They asked each other, "What qualities make someone a good friend?" They thought about the many things they had learned from Character Links that made each of them a good friend.

Misifu said, "First, you have to use your imagination to be able to have empathy for someone. Remember when Moo-Moo had her leg broken? You and I have never had a broken leg, but using our imaginations, we could imagine how difficult it was for her to be on crutches and unable to run and play."

John Louie said, "You have to be caring, and you have to turn that care and concern into action. Remember when Chadwick showed his caring by physically pulling Moo-Moo to and from school in his red wagon after her accident?" Misifu did remember.

Misifu continued, "To be a good friend, it's important to be a good listener. You are a good friend when you don't tell anyone else the personal things that I share with you. When I told you that I was frightened by some scary Halloween decorations, you didn't say, 'That's silly.' You listened and respected my feelings, even though the decorations didn't frighten you. I can trust you, John Louie."

John Louie said, "I can share my opinions with you. When I said I didn't like vegetables, you didn't lecture me on the nutritional importance of vegetables. You just listened, nodding and looking directly at me when I was talking. I knew you were listening and paying attention. Even when you don't agree with me, you try to understand and don't give me advice unless I ask. Later, when I told you I liked fresh corn, you just smiled."

Misifu added, "Being respectful is important. You never interrupt when I'm talking, John Louie. Taking turns and sharing is also part of being a good friend. Friends work together accomplishing tasks that are difficult to do alone. Remember when you shared with me your idea of building a secret hiding place? We worked together building it, and now we both enjoy playing in our secret hiding place."

John Louie was willing to share Misifu with other kittens. He wasn't jealous when she spent time with other friends. They listed together the qualities necessary to be a good friend. It was necessary to have imagination and empathy, and to be caring, trustworthy, a good listener, and willing to take turns and share. They both said in unison:

"There's nothing so precious, nothing so valuable as a good friend."

ACTIVITIES

Questions to promote interaction and understanding of this Character Link:

- Why do you think that Misifu and John Louie were good friends?

- How are imagination and empathy related?

- How would you know how someone felt? Suggestions: Look at their face. Look at their body language. Listen to the tone of their voice. What would you do to help them?

- Why is it important to be caring?

- When you want to be a good friend, how important is it to listen?

- How did John Louie show he was trustworthy when Misifu told him about her fears?

- Why is it important to not give advice unless it is asked for?

- Why is being respectful a necessary quality?

- How did Misifu act when John Louie said, "I don't like vegetables"?

- How did Misifu act when John Louie changed his mind and shared with Misifu that he now liked corn?

- How did John Louie act when Misifu was talking?

- Why is *not interrupting* so important, not only with friends but with everyone?

- Why is sharing an important part of friendship?

- What does being "jealous" mean to you?

- Why did Misifu and John Louie say together, "There's nothing so precious, nothing so valuable as a good friend"?

Invite the children to name someone they consider a good friend. Ask, "What qualities can you identify in your friend? What qualities do *you* have that also make you a good friend?"

Ask the children how they feel about sharing their friend with others.

If any of the children are having difficulty with one of the qualities (one of the Character Links) of friendship, ask if they would like help. Work with them to think of an exercise that will help them acquire that quality.

25

I ENJOY ALONE TIME

25 I ENJOY ALONE TIME

To *enjoy* means to get pleasure from something. *Alone time* means the time you spend all by yourself, away from other people.

Chadwick lay on his cushion, enjoying the solitude. It was so peaceful. When he was in his special place, his thoughts would not be interrupted by anything or anybody.

He could daydream. Daydreaming allowed him to go anywhere he wanted to go.

Chadwick's mother had told him he was now old enough to learn to swim. He could hardly wait to get started. He dreamed of winning a gold medal in the summer Olympics. He saw himself wearing the gold medal on the colorful ribbon, proudly standing on the awards platform. A tear of joy ran down his furry cheek as the national anthem was played. The cheers and applause surrounded him.

His thoughts then went to the Character Links. He recited the poem:

Character Links, Character Links,
There seem to be so many!
But, master one and then go on
And soon you'll master many.

Chadwick remembered the very first Character Link, "I am responsible," and smiled. It seemed so long ago. He was so much more responsible now. He had experienced a lot of personal changes since he first started. He celebrated, in his mind, all of his past successes. He felt good about his efforts. The good feelings made him want to keep learning and mastering all of the Character Links. He wondered how long it would take to complete them all.

His birthday was approaching. He daydreamed about what he would like to do and whom he would invite to his party. They could play tag, count bugs, and chase butterflies. They could play pin the tail on the dog. They could have boxes filled with things to touch, without looking, and then guess what it was that they were feeling. It would be fun to have a pinata, filled with things that kittens would enjoy, things like catnip mice, shrimp rolls, sardines, and anchovy popcorn. There could be balls with bells inside, and feather toys to chase. He would share his daydream with his mother, and together they would plan his party.

Chadwick must have fallen asleep during his alone time, because the next sound he heard was the dinner bell. He got up, stretched his longest cat stretch, and hurried to dinner on his four little paws.

John Louie **enjoys alone time** to daydream without interruption.

ACTIVITIES

Questions to promote interaction and understanding of this Character Link:

- Why did Chadwick enjoy his alone time?
- Why is it important to daydream?
- What could he see himself winning in the future?
- What made him recite the Character Link poem?
- What was the value for Chadwick of remembering the experiences that he had when he started learning the Character Links?
- Why did he enjoy celebrating all of his past successes?
- What is the value of remembering past successes?
- How did he feel about learning the remaining Character Links?
- When he was daydreaming, what was he thinking about?
- How was he going to use the daydream to plan his party?
- How did he feel when his alone time was over?

How can you create a special place for alone time? Help the children think of possibilities:

- A large cardboard box with cutout windows and a door.
- A blanket stretched over two chairs.
- A quiet corner in a room, without noise and distractions.
- A cushion in a sunny bay window.
- A grassy spot under the shade of a large tree.
- A corner in a garden.
- Your own room.

Add to this list all the possibilities suggested by the children.

Share with the children that after they have found a physical spot for alone time, they can also create a special place in their minds. They should choose a special place that makes them feel happy and relaxed. Help the children create their special place in their mind. Possibilities might be:

- A favorite sandy beach near the ocean.
- A beautiful castle.
- A leafy den in the middle of the forest.
- A warm sunny spot near a lake.
- Near a good-fairy princess.
- A location from a scene in one of your favorite movies.
- Floating on a large, white, puffy cloud.
- A comfortable resting spot on dozens of lavender and pink cushions or cushions of their own favorite colors.

Add to this brief list all the special places thought up by the children.

After deciding on a physical location and picking your mind's special place, what can you choose to do in your special location during alone time? Here are a few possibilities:

- Daydream about anything.
- Look at a beautiful book.
- Play with your favorite toys.
- Take a nap.
- Make believe you are whatever you want to be.

Add to this all of the suggestions the children offer. The suggestions they make may be helpful to others who are having difficulty with this exercise.

26

I HAVE AN OPEN MIND

26   I HAVE AN OPEN MIND

> An *open mind* means a mind that is not closed or shut. Having an open mind means being able to take in new ideas, facts, or beliefs.

Chadwick's dad was readying his fishing gear. He had a fishing pole, bait, and a net to scoop the fish out of the water. Chadwick could see that his father was excited. Chadwick didn't much like fishing—you had to be too quiet and still. He was learning to be patient, but fishing required more patience than he had. Chadwick liked action.

His dad said, "Let's go fishing!"

Chadwick replied, "It's not much fun if I don't have someone to play with."

His dad said, "Keep an open mind, Chadwick. Something fun always happens. I'm making catfish sandwiches for our picnic, and anchovy popcorn for dessert." Chadwick felt a little better, because he loved catfish sandwiches and anchovy popcorn.

Then Chadwick looked outside and saw a gloomy, overcast sky. "But Dad, it's going to rain. We can't have a picnic in the rain."

His father replied, "You don't think so? Chadwick, it sounds like your mind is closed to the possibilities. We could take a tent. Or, if it's too wet, we could eat inside our cozy van. There are lots of ways to have a picnic in the rain. Besides, we don't know for sure that it will rain. Maybe the skies will clear."

With little enthusiasm, Chadwick climbed in the van for the trip to the lake. As they were driving, the sky started to brighten and the sun suddenly broke through the overcast. Perhaps his dad was right about keeping an open mind. The weather was changing for the better.

As his dad sat by the edge of the lake, fishing pole in his paws, Chadwick decided to explore. He hadn't gone far when he spotted Lettuce in the distance. His dad was right again about keeping an open mind. Now he had found a playmate.

Lettuce the turtle was one of Chadwick's very good friends. Chadwick laughed at himself on the way over to greet him. He remembered how annoyed he had been the first time he played with Lettuce because the little turtle walked so s-l-o-w-l-y. Since becoming friends, how s-l-o-w-l-y Lettuce walked no longer bothered him.

As Chadwick approached, Lettuce called out, "I challenge you to race me to the end of the lake." Chadwick gleefully accepted the challenge.

Chadwick couldn't help feeling superior. He knew that he would win any race because Lettuce walked so s-l-o-w-l-y. They both started off around the lake.

After a short distance, when a butterfly crossed the path, Chadwick gave chase. The butterfly flitted from one flowering bush to the next, always leaving just as Chadwick leaped to capture it. The chase continued for some time. Chadwick was tiring of all this jumping and leaping, so he decided to return to the path and continue the race. A butterfly flew behind him just as he reached the path. He made one last leap but missed the butterfly.

Turning around on the path he glanced toward the end of the lake. Much to his amazement, he watched

Lettuce s-l-o-w-l-y walk out of the water and across the finish line.

Chadwick ran over to congratulate him. "Knowing how slowly you walk, it's awesome. I left the path to chase a butterfly. I never considered for a minute that you could win a race with me. My dad and I talked about the importance of having an open mind. I forgot to keep an open mind—open to the possibility that you might swim to the end of the lake! I lost the race because I had a closed mind."

Talking with his dad about keeping an open mind wasn't enough. Chadwick needed to learn to keep an open mind in real-life situations. Just because he was a cat who didn't like getting wet, he forgot that Lettuce the turtle loved to swim. His mistake taught him a valuable lesson.

Chadwick invited Lettuce to join their picnic. He removed the lettuce from his catfish sandwich and gave it to his friend. After all, the turtle had been named Lettuce because lettuce was his favorite food.

> Chadwick realized the importance of keeping an **open mind** when his s-l-o-w friend Lettuce surprised him and won the race.

ACTIVITIES

Questions to promote interaction and understanding of this Character Link:

- Why do you think Chadwick's father wanted him to appreciate the difference between a "closed mind" and an "open mind?"
- Why was Chadwick no longer annoyed with Lettuce because he walked s-l-o-w-l-y?
- When you get to know someone, does that sometimes change your feelings about them?
- When Chadwick felt superior to Lettuce, how did he feel?
- What happened to Chadwick when he knew that he would win the race?
- How important was it for Chadwick to be focused on the goal of winning the race?
- What made Chadwick lose sight of the goal of winning the race?
- What happened when he got distracted?
- When Chadwick returned to the path, what did he see?
- Why is it important to keep an open mind?
- What do you think some people prefer to keep a closed mind? (It's easier; they don't have to think. They don't have to process new information—they never allow it to enter their minds. They feel safer, more secure, "knowing" they are right.)

The caregiver, teacher, or children bring to the group several ethnic foods from different cultures. These could be dishes eaten in their homes. Consider including unusual fruits such as starfruit, kiwi, pomegranates, and persimmons, cut up into small pieces. Invite the children to taste the different foods. If a child says, "I don't want to," respect that. If a child says, "I don't like that," it provides an opportunity to ask how it tastes to him or her.

It's important to point out that when people say, "I don't like it," and then later admit that they have never tasted it, that this is an example of a closed mind.

When someone is willing to try a new food, that exhibits the behavior of having an open mind. That person is open to the possibility of discovering something new. If after tasting the food some children still say, "I don't like it," then everyone should respect their opinions because they have exhibited the courage to try the new food.

You might comment to the children that our tastes change with time. Encourage them to always keep an open mind to the possibility of tasting something again, at a later time, to see if their opinion has changed.

27

I AM SELF-DISCIPLINED

27   I AM SELF-DISCIPLINED

> Being *self-disciplined* means doing what you know is right, even when there is no parent, teacher, caregiver, or police officer watching you. It also means you are able to develop new skills, good character, and good habits.

Misifu's mother had asked her to always wash her paws before eating and especially after using the litter box. Misifu tried to remember, but she really didn't understand the importance of it all. Her mother said, "There are germs on your paws. You don't want those germs in your mouth, or on things that you handle, or on the food you eat."

Misifu held her paws up and examined them very carefully, looking for something crawling around. She looked and looked but couldn't see anything. Sometimes she remembered to wash her paws, but sometimes she didn't.

Her birthday was coming up. Misifu's mother asked her if she would like to go to a cat restaurant that had just opened. If she wanted, she could invite her friend John Louie to join them. Her mother said, "I think you'll like it, and the food is supposed to be excellent."

Misifu replied, "I would like to go somewhere special to celebrate my birthday. I'll call John Louie and ask if he can come."

John Louie accepted the invitation. He had a cold, but he wasn't sneezing anymore. Misifu was such a good friend that he didn't want to miss her party.

The restaurant was beautifully decorated. It had sparkles on the walls and colorfully painted wall coverings and candles. The restaurant had a long menu.

Misifu and John Louie didn't know what to order. Misifu's mother asked questions about what they would like, and she ordered for them.

They had anchovy rolls for an appetizer, catnip salad with sardine dressing, and an entree of fresh tuna on a bed of crispy shrimp. It was delicious. For dessert there was whipped cream. They were stuffed and had a wonderful evening. John Louie was very well mannered and passed everything to Misifu and her parents.

Misifu awoke several days later with a terrible cold. Her nose was stuffy and she could hardly breathe. Her mother was very loving and brought her warm milk and soup and some of her favorite fish crackers. She took the opportunity to talk with Misifu about the importance of washing your paws—especially when you have a cold. John Louie had given his cold to Misifu because of the germs on his hands when he passed food to her at the restaurant.

Now Misifu had a better understanding of what germs were all about. After she recovered from her cold, she had no trouble remembering to wash her paws. In a kind way, she would share this information with John Louie. She knew he would never mean to give her or anyone else something unpleasant. You can't see germs, but some germs have very unpleasant effects.

> Misifu is **self-disciplined** when she remembers
> to wash her paws before eating.

ACTIVITIES

Questions to promote interaction and understanding of this Character Link:

- Why did Misifu's mother ask her to wash her paws before eating and after using the litter box?
- What Character Links did Misifu's mother demonstrate when she asked Misifu if she wanted to invite John Louie to her birthday dinner?
- Why did John Louie accept the invitation?
- What kind of an evening did they have?
- When John Louie was passing food, what else was he also passing?
- How did Misifu feel several days later when her nose was stuffy?
- What did her mother explain to her about passing germs when you have a cold?
- When did Misifu appreciate the importance of washing her paws?
- How was she going to share her new knowledge about this with John Louie?
- How was she being a good friend when she shared this information with John Louie?
- What did Misifu think about germs?
- How did this change her behavior?

Being self-disciplined means making good choices and practicing good habits. What are some good habits that are important to learn? Here are some examples:

- Washing our hands.
- Brushing our teeth.
- Going to bed on time.
- Eating healthy foods.
- Being honest.
- Being trustworthy.
- Being respectful.
- Being responsible.
- Using good manners.
- Thinking before acting.
- Being patient.
- Considering the feelings of others.
- Evaluating personal experiences.
- Enjoying alone time.
- Developing imagination.
- Sharing with others.
- Working with others.
- Being a good listener.

How do we learn good habits? (By practicing over and over and over making good choices.) Habits represent who you are.

28

I KNOW HOW TO ASK
FOR WHAT I NEED

28 I KNOW HOW TO ASK FOR WHAT I NEED

> *Knowing how to ask* means not being afraid to ask for something. *What you need* is something that you feel is very important to you.

Pushpa sat on the floor watching her mother prepare dinner. She felt lonely and needy.

She had been to kitten school that day and completed her assignments. After school, she was invited to a friend's home. Other kittens from school had been invited as well. Everyone was having a good time.

Everything went well until someone suggested playing tag. Her friend's home had hardwood floors and they were very slippery for her furry Persian paws. Whenever Pushpa turned a corner at high speed, her feet flew out from under her. She had so much fur between her toes that running on wood floors was like skating on ice.

Several kittens, not Persians, teased her. "You can't stand up!" they said. "You can't stand up!" It hurt her feelings. Being teased was not pleasant.

When she returned home, Pushpa wanted to be held by her mother. She wanted to be kissed on her pink nose and assured that she was fine just as she was—slippery furry feet and all.

Her mother looked very busy making dinner. What would her mother say if Pushpa interrupted the dinner preparation? Would her mother think she was being silly? Pushpa didn't feel silly. Would her mother think that Pushpa was being too sensitive? She continued to think about it. She thought that the worst that could happen would be to hear a big "No, I don't have time right now."

Pushpa continued thinking and thinking about it, finally deciding that it was worth the risk. She walked over to her mother and tugged on her apron. It took a lot of courage when she said in a very small voice, "I really need a hug. I was teased a lot after school, because I kept falling down when we were playing tag. The wooden floors were too slippery for my furry Persian paws."

Her mother stopped, put down her bowl, and picked her up. She kissed Pushpa's pink nose and the pink bottoms of her furry paws. She whispered in her ear, "You're a perfect kitten, just as you are."

Pushpa felt warm and wonderful all over. Next time she wouldn't hesitate to share her feelings and ask for what she needed.

When Pushpa sadly told her mother, "I need a hug!" **she knew how to ask for what she needed.**

ACTIVITIES

Questions to promote interaction and understanding of this Character Link:

- Why did Pushpa feel lonely and needy?
- What did the other kittens do that hurt her feelings?
- Which Character Link had these kittens not learned?
- What did Pushpa want from her mother?
- When Pushpa was watching her mother in the kitchen, what was she thinking?
- What Character Link did Pushpa need in order to ask for what she needed?
- How did she get her mother's attention?
- What Character Link did Pushpa's mother demonstrate when she stopped working?
- How did Pushpa feel after her mother set down her mixing bowl and picked her up?

When you say, "I need the red crayon," how does this need differ from the need that Pushpa expressed?

When you say, "I need a Band-Aid," is this the kind of need that Pushpa expressed?

When you ask for a Barbie Mobile Home, is this the kind of need Pushpa was expressing?

What kind of need was Pushpa talking about?

You can learn a new word. The kind of need that Pushpa expressed is a *psychological* need. The word is pronounced psy-cho-log-i-cal. What does the word mean? It means a feeling in your mind.

What kind of need do you think is the most difficult to express? A need for a drink of water or food, an object, a toy, a stuffed animal? Or . . .

- A need for a hug?
- A need for encouragement?
- A need to feel you belong?
- A need to be accepted?
- A need to believe in your own goodness?
- A need to be loved?
- A need to be listened to?
- A need to feel needed, valued, and important?
- A need to feel fairly treated?

Why do you think that is so?

What must you have before you can ask for anything? (For example, you need to feel good about yourself, and you need to have courage to take the risk of asking.)

29

I APPRECIATE HUMOR

29   I APPRECIATE HUMOR

To *appreciate* means to understand the value of something and to be thankful for it. *Humor* means things that are funny and that make you laugh.

Chadwick and his friend, Pepe the mouse, sat side by side in the big circus tent. They loved the clowns and all the performing animals. Elephants were their favorite. A purple elephant was already on stage when a tiny hot pink mouse entered the ring. "And now," said the ringmaster, "make way for the strongest mouse in the world!"

The little mouse flexed his muscles and puffed out his chest. The elephant seemed to smile. In an instant, the mouse flipped the purple elephant over his head and lifted him high into the air.

Chadwick and Pepe just stared. It was amazing! They believed their eyes, even though what they had just seen was impossible. But wait—was that a hissing sound? As they listened, the hissing grew louder and louder. At the same time, the elephant was getting smaller and smaller. What could be happening? The crowd watched the purple elephant collapse into folds and wrinkles. Soon he was as flat as a pancake. The purple elephant had been a huge balloon. The mouse wasn't the strongest mouse in the world—he was a clown! Pepe and Chadwick laughed so hard that tears rolled down their cheeks. They stood and cheered for the hot pink mouse.

After the show, Chadwick and Pepe talked about how much fun it had been, and how good it felt to laugh. "I wish we could laugh like that every day," Pepe said.

Chadwick turned thoughtful, "You know, sometimes we have to be careful about laughing," he told Pepe. "Yesterday I was laughing at my friend Pushpa, and it hurt her feelings. Humor should never be used to hurt someone."

Chadwick explained what had happened. A group of kittens were playing tag, and Pushpa couldn't stand up. When she tried to turn a corner, her feet would fly out in all directions. Then—WHOOPS—she would fall down. She looked very silly. It made the other kittens laugh. They were so busy laughing, they forgot to think about Pushpa's feelings. When Pushpa stopped playing, Chadwick wondered why she looked so sad. "What's wrong?" he asked.

Pushpa lifted one of her paws. "See all the fur between my toes? That's why I slide and lose my footing." She could run like the wind on soft carpeting, but not on slippery wooden floors. Chadwick looked at his own paws. He didn't have fur between his toes, so it was easy for him to run anywhere.

"I learned an important lesson," Chadwick told Pepe. "Not everyone is alike, but it's not OK to laugh at their differences. Laughing is no fun at all when it hurts someone's feelings. Laughter is best when we can all do it together!"

> Chadwick and Pepe **appreciate the humor** of the pink mouse
> who is really a clown, and the huge purple elephant
> who is really just a balloon.

ACTIVITIES

Questions to promote interaction and understanding of this Character Link:

- What was the reaction of Pepe and Chadwick when the pink mouse flipped the purple elephant over his head?
- What made them laugh so hard that tears rolled down their cheeks?
- Why is laughter such a wonderful experience?
- Why did Chadwick say you have to be careful about laughing?
- How did Pushpa feel when the kittens laughed at her?
- Why did she stop playing?
- Why did Chadwick tell Pepe, "Not everyone is alike, but it's not OK to laugh at their differences"?
- What does it mean when we say, "Never use humor as a weapon"?
- Why is it important to always consider the feelings of others?
- Why is it better when everyone can laugh together, and no one is left out?

In a circle, ask the children to name some of the things that they laugh at.

Ask the children to give examples of laughter that might hurt someone's feelings.

Ask the children to think of activities that the entire group can laugh at and enjoy. An example would be the following:

One child stands behind another child. The child in front holds his or her arms in back so that they don't show. The person in front does all the talking and makes faces. The child in back extends his or her arms in front of the first person and makes all the hand movements. The children who are watching call out activities for these two to act out. Examples: brushing their teeth, eating a sandwich, washing their hands, and washing the dishes.

Have the children do a humorous hand puppet show or dress up in costumes and act out a funny skit.

Have the children bring videos taken with their family. Fast-forward the movie and then play the movie in reverse.

Have a clown entertain the group.

Obtain a book of jokes appropriate for children and share several with them.

Read a humorous story that the children can enjoy.

30

I PERSEVERE

30 I PERSEVERE

> To *persevere* means to keep trying, and to continue faithfully and steadily, without letting anything get in your way.

Liang enjoyed watching the runners in the local races. She often helped at the events by passing out water along the race route. Liang thought that someday she would like to be in a race. She thought that wearing a number and being cheered on by the crowd would be wonderful.

The morning after one race, she mentioned her idea to her mother. Liang's mother smiled and said, "Remember that succeeding at any endeavor requires a great deal of work and perseverance. Perseverance means sticking to your goal even when you don't feel like it. Anyone who does something well makes it look easy. However, it's difficult for everyone in the beginning. If you really want to be a runner, how about starting your training tomorrow, before school?"

Liang enthusiastically replied, "Yes, I'll do that!" It meant getting up earlier, but Liang was excited.

The next morning, her mother helped her tie the laces on her running shoes. "Start slowly, Liang," her mother said. "Just go around our block. I'll have breakfast ready when you return."

Liang started out enthusiastically. One quarter of the way around the block, she was running out of breath. Halfway around, her paws were getting tired. Three quarters of the way around, she wondered if she would make it home. She admired runners even *more* now. She was beginning to understand the effort involved.

Her legs were like jelly as she walked into the kitchen. Her mom gave her a hug and offered encouragement. "The hard part is to persevere when you find out how difficult running can be."

Every morning Liang's mother gave her a hug and helped her tie the laces of her running shoes. And every day, her mother wrote down how far Liang ran and how long it took her, so that Liang could see her progress.

After three weeks, she breathed more easily. Her paws and legs became stronger. She ran just a little further each day. Within a month she was running around the block five times each morning. In two months, she was running around the block ten times. After three months, she was running much faster and ran around the block thirty times each morning.

When Liang signed up for her first race, she placed in the top ten. "Next time, I want to win," Liang said.

Her mother smiled and said, "Remember, perseverance wins!"

> Liang learned to **persevere** when she was training to be a runner.

ACTIVITIES

Questions to promote interaction and understanding of this Character Link:

- How did Liang become interested in running?
- What was the most important thing Liang did in the very beginning?
- What did she like about running?
- What did Liang's mother tell her about succeeding?
- How did Liang's mother support her when she set her goal?
- What did Liang quickly find out about persevering?
- Why did she admire runners even more after she started?
- What did her mother do to help her see her progress?
- After Liang had practiced for several weeks, what did she do?
- How did she do in her first race?
- When the race was over, why did Liang's mother say, "Remember, perseverance wins"?

Why is the Character Link *I am patient* important to someone who is learning to persevere?

Invite the children to name something that they presently can't do, but they would like to learn to do. Make a list of all the things named by the children. The list might include things like these:

- Learning to control a pencil.
- Learning to swim.
- Learning to be a ballerina.
- Learning one of the Character Links.
- Learning to tie a shoelace.
- Learning to be a play director.
- Learning to ride a bicycle.
- Learning to play a musical instrument.
- Learning to bake delicious cookies.
- Learning to read.

Invite the children to suggest important steps to reach the goal that they have selected. How will they decide the first important step?

Who would they like to have supporting their efforts?

When selecting someone to support you, why is it important to find someone with the Character Link of *empathy*? Why is it important to find someone who has incorporated the Character Link of *respect*?

Why is the Character Link *I am what I believe* important to perseverance? What influence does this Character Link have on your success?

What role does *perseverance* play in your finally reaching your goal?

31

I AM CAPABLE

31   I AM CAPABLE

> Being *capable* means having a particular ability or skill,
> or being able to do something well.

John Louie was fascinated by goldfish and their movements. He liked the way that light reflected off their scales. Sometimes they looked iridescent. When he first started visiting their bowl, they would hide. Over time, they realized that he meant them no harm and they began to trust him. In fact, they seemed pleased to see him when he visited. They had to be fed daily and as John Louie grew up, he wanted to be the one to feed them.

When Heather thought he was old enough and his paws large enough, she showed him how to hold the container and gently shake the food into the bowl.

He was so excited. The day he had been waiting for was finally here. John Louie was going to feed the goldfish! He held the container as he had been shown, but he shook it so hard that it flew out of his paws and into the goldfish bowl. Water splashed out of the bowl and large waves hit against the sides. The goldfish were terrified and hid behind the seaweed.

A tear rolled down John Louie's cheek. He felt just terrible. Heather gave him a reassuring paw pat. With a small net, she lifted the container of food from the bowl. She carefully dried off the container and then asked John Louie to pick it up. She suggested that he shake it gently this time.

John Louie was afraid he would drop it again. He was afraid to try again. He didn't want to scare the fish again. They were his friends. Heather said, "I know you are afraid, but I will stay very close to you. I know you can do it this time."

John Louie picked up the container and gently shook the food into the bowl, with Heather standing patiently at his side. This time he was successful.

Heather told him that when anyone is learning something new, it is impossible to do it perfectly at first. It takes courage to become capable. Learning is a process. Only by continuing to try would John Louie become a capable cat.

> By carefully scattering the right amount of food for the goldfish, John Louie showed he is **capable** of feeding them.

ACTIVITIES

Questions to promote interaction and understanding of this Character Link:

- How did John Louie feel about the goldfish?
- How did the goldfish feel about John Louie when he first started watching them?
- Why were the goldfish nervous?
- What Character Link did John Louie need to demonstrate if he was going to gain their trust?
- When did Heather decide it was time for John Louie to learn how to feed the goldfish?
- How did she begin his training?
- Why was John Louie excited?
- What happened when he first tried?
- How did Heather react?
- What did she do that encouraged John Louie to try again?
- Why did Heather say it was impossible to do something perfectly the first time he tried?
- What Character Link did John Louie possess that was important to his trying again?

What are the qualities necessary for someone to become capable? (The following Character Links apply.)

I am patient.

I am a good listener.

I am courageous.

I enjoy learning.

I am curious.

I am actively involved in life.

I have an open mind.

I am self-disciplined.

I persevere.

I have a positive attitude.

Why are these qualities necessary?

What are some of the obstacles that you will encounter when you are attempting to learn a skill?

In what areas would you like to become capable?

32

I BELIEVE THERE IS AN ABUNDANCE OF LOVE IN MY WORLD

32   I BELIEVE THERE IS AN ABUNDANCE OF LOVE IN MY WORLD

To *believe* means to have a feeling that something is true. *Abundance* means a very large amount—even more than you need. *Love* is a strong, warm feeling for another. People who *love* you care deeply about you, believe in you, and think you are a valuable person.

Pushpa's mother told her, "Being loving is a choice. Looking for the good in people is a choice. Affection is learned when you are a kitten. Choose friends that are loving and joyous."

Pushpa had been picked up, hugged, and kissed on the end of her pink nose and the bottoms of her pink, furry paws for as long as she could remember. Now she found herself hugging and kissing her kitten friends, and even Pepe the mouse, who was a friend of all the kittens. She hugged Pepe and kissed him on the end of his pink nose and the bottoms of his tiny pink feet.

Pushpa's mother was always there for her when she needed her. Pushpa learned that love means being there when you're needed. When Pushpa started painting, her mother was full of love and encouragement, even when others laughed at the idea of a cat painter. All this love and encouragement helped her keep on doing what she loved to do and helped her be successful.

Her mother always used the language of love when she spoke with Pushpa. She always tried her best to understand Pushpa, and when she didn't understand, she asked questions. Her mother was interested in knowing what was happening in Pushpa's life and how she was affected by

it—like the time she was teased for falling down on the slippery wood floors.

Because Pushpa had received so much love from her family and in school, she was able to give love to all of her kitten friends and the adult cats in her life. She was able to share and enjoy their successes. When Misifu and Moo-Moo built their sand castle with the help of Chipie and Hedgie, Pushpa celebrated. When John Louie learned to feed the goldfish, Pushpa celebrated his accomplishment. Because of her loving attitude, everyone enjoyed being with Pushpa.

Pushpa found that the more love she gave away, the more love surrounded her. The more love she received, the more creative and joyous she became.

She took risks and gave love to everyone. Sometimes her love wasn't appreciated. Some older cats had difficulty accepting love. At first, it hurt Pushpa's feelings when her love was rejected. However, she was quick to forgive when her feelings were hurt. She felt empathy for the cats who couldn't accept love and pushed her away. They hadn't been loved as kittens, and when they grew up they didn't know how to give love to others. Also they were unable to accept love themselves. That saddened Pushpa.

Pushpa kept hugging and loving everyone around her. Pushpa knew that her life was a series of moments, and she wasn't going to waste any of them. Being loved had made her loving. She hoped that being loving would make others loving. She celebrated the joy of loving and being loved every day.

Pushpa **believes** that there is an **abundance of love** to be received from parents, brothers and sisters, grandparents, relatives, teachers, friends, caregivers, nannies, pets, and most importantly, from herself.

ACTIVITIES

Questions to promote interaction and understanding of this Character Link:

- What did Pushpa's mother mean when she said, "Being loving is a choice"?
- What did she mean when she said, "Looking for the good in people is a choice"?
- What is the foundation for being loving?
- How do you learn to be loving?
- What was the importance of Pushpa being hugged and kissed as a kitten?
- Why is "being there when needed" an important part of being loving?
- Why was Pushpa able to share and enjoy other kittens' successes?
- When Pushpa gave love away, what happened?
- What happened when she gave love away and she was rejected?
- How important is it to be able to forgive?
- How did Pushpa feel about people who couldn't accept love?
- Why did she keep giving love away?

What are ways that you can make the world more loving? List all the suggestions from the children.

Starting today, what are some ways to start expressing a more loving attitude at school? Invite every child to make a contribution by saying:

> "*Today*, I shall be more loving at school by _____."
>
> "*Today*, I shall be more loving at home by _____."

In the following days, discuss the reactions they have gotten to their efforts at school and at home.

Have the children repeat:

Character Links, Character Links,
There seem to be so many!
But master one and then go on
And soon you'll master many.

33

I HAVE A POSITIVE ATTITUDE

33   I HAVE A POSITIVE ATTITUDE

> *Attitude* means a way of thinking, acting, or feeling. Having a *positive attitude* means always seeing the good side of things.

When Chadwick was a young kitten, lapping cream from a saucer, his mother asked him to tell her whether his saucer of cream was half full or half empty. Chadwick stopped lapping the cream. He looked at the dish. He said, "It could be half full, or it could be half empty." From his position, he thought either answer could be right. The answer depended on how he looked at it.

His mother answered, "You are absolutely right, Chadwick. If you said the saucer was half full, you would be right. If you said the saucer was half empty, you would also be right. Why do you think I asked you the question?"

Chadwick said, "Because you wanted me to know that there's more than one way to look at a situation?"

"True," replied his mother. "I also want you to understand the importance of choosing the answer that is best for you. If you choose *half empty*, how does that make you feel?"

Chadwick thought before answering. "It makes me worry. What will happen when the saucer is empty? I feel that there isn't enough. Will I be hungry when it's gone?"

His mother smiled. "And if you look at the saucer as half full, how do you feel?"

"That's easier," said Chadwick. "I feel better. I'm grateful that my saucer is half full. It means I still have lots of cream to drink."

Chadwick definitely knew that his attitude determined the outcome. He had only to remember the race he had with Lettuce, the turtle. Because Lettuce walked so s-l-o-w-l-y, Chadwick, with an air of superiority, "knew" he would win the race.

Well, Lettuce had a positive attitude. He knew that he could swim much faster than he could walk. After the race had started and Chadwick was off chasing butterflies, Lettuce had slipped into the water. Instead of trying to run, he swam to the end of the lake. He s-l-o-w-l-y walked across the finish line and won the race while Chadwick watched from the path. Lettuce was a perfect example of someone with a positive attitude.

Chadwick decided to write a funny poem to remind him of this Character Link:

> *If the option arises to choose*
> *Whether to win or to lose*
> *Skip the negative, snegative*
> *Choose the positive wozitive.*

Chadwick has a **positive attitude** when he sees his saucer
of cream as half full, rather than half empty.

ACTIVITIES

Questions to promote interaction and understanding of this Character Link:

- What question did Chadwick's mother ask him when he was lapping cream from his saucer?
- Why do you think she asked Chadwick this question?
- What did Chadwick learn from being asked this question?
- Why was she concerned that Chadwick learn to choose the answer that was best for him?
- When he thought his saucer was half empty, how did he feel?
- When he thought his saucer was half full, how did he feel?
- What does it mean when we say, "Chadwick knew that *his attitude determined the outcome*"?
- What attitude did Chadwick have when Lettuce invited him to race?
- What attitude did Chadwick have after the race was over?
- What was the difference?
- How was the attitude of Lettuce the turtle?
- Why do you think Chadwick wrote his funny poem?

    If the option arises to choose

    Whether to win or to lose

    Skip the negative, snegative

    Choose the positive wozitive.

Who knows what *attitude* means? Attitude means a way of thinking, acting, or feeling. It's important to understand the difference between having a positive attitude or having a negative attitude. After each of these sentences, say whether the attitude expressed is *positive* or *negative:*

- I'm afraid to ride my bicycle. I might fall off and be hurt.
- I like riding my bicycle.
- Being curious gets me in trouble.
- When I'm curious I learn new things.
- I don't care what people think of my behavior.
- Manners are important because people appreciate someone who is polite.
- School is boring.
- I enjoy school because I learn new things.
- I don't like helping because I'd rather watch television.
- I like helping my mother.

What happens when we make a positive statement and then add "but _____"? Here is a sentence that illustrates this:

"Thank you for returning the toys to the toy box, but you forgot to put away the yellow blocks."

How did you feel about the first part of the sentence, before the *but?*

How did you feel after the *but* was added to the sentence?

How does this Character Link remind you of an earlier Character Link, "I choose my own thoughts"?

Why is it so important to remember to be patient with ourselves when we are attempting to learn, "I have a positive attitude"?

34

I AM COURAGEOUS

34   I AM COURAGEOUS

> Being *courageous* means being brave when you face fear, danger, or great difficulty.

Chadwick stood by the edge of the pool, terrified. The thought of jumping into the water filled him with fear. What if he couldn't breathe? What if his mother didn't catch him? What if he drowned? His visions of disaster were unending. He was focused on fear.

His mother waited patiently in the water, offering words of encouragement. Until this moment, she had always supported Chadwick in the water, holding him in her arms to make him feel safe. He knew nothing bad could ever happen to him when he was in his mother's arms.

Standing at the edge of the pool all by himself was an entirely different matter. He felt paralyzed. It looked like miles from the edge of the pool to the water. He felt like he was going to fall hundreds of feet before he would be in his mother's arms.

He stood and stood and stood. He wanted to be courageous, but his fear was holding him back. His mother smiled and said, "Chadwick, you'll never learn to swim by standing at the edge of the pool. I know you are frightened. I'd never let anything happen to you. You're too precious. The only way to overcome fear is to confront it!"

She opened her arms to Chadwick and said, "Acknowledge the fear and then focus on your goal of learning to swim. It takes a leap of faith. I know that you are courageous. You've met many challenges before—remember when you learned to ride your bicycle? You have to acknowledge the fear, and then use that energy to work through it. It is so important to learn to swim. Sometime, I may not be here. If you know how to swim, you'll always be safe near the pool."

Chadwick took a deep breath. Using all the courage he had, he jumped into the water. As his head went under the water, he could feel his whiskers floating. His mother picked him up as he rose to the surface.

It wasn't as bad as he had imagined. In fact, it was wonderful. He had done it! He had met fear straight on. There would be many lessons to master before he could swim independently, but he had overcome his fear. Fear had also given him the energy to finally jump. Chadwick understood the true meaning of *I am courageous!*

> Chadwick was **courageous** when he was afraid of the water
> but jumped into the pool anyway.

ACTIVITIES

Questions to promote interaction and understanding of this Character Link:

- What was the emotion that Chadwick was experiencing?
- How was he using his imagination in a negative way?
- Why did he feel paralyzed?
- What prevented him from being courageous?
- How did his mother react to him?
- Why did she remind him of times when he had been courageous before?
- Why did his mother feel that it was important for him to learn how to swim?
- What quality did Chadwick's mother have that helped him?
- How did he feel about continuing with swimming lessons?
- How did he feel about the experience?
- What gave him the energy to jump? (His fear, trust in his mother, and his mother's encouragement.)
- What is another name for courage? (Being brave.)

What does being *discouraged* mean? It means losing our courage. Who is willing to share a time when you felt discouraged?

How did you regain your courage?

Who helped you when you were discouraged?

Why is it important to celebrate your smallest successes?

Invite the children to share a time when they were really frightened. What did they do about it?

Some children pull the covers over their head and hide when they have a nightmare. Other children have a more positive approach. For example, they might ask for help from parents to get rid of the character in their nightmare. They think of ways to deal with the nightmare, just as Chadwick did in the Character Link, "I choose my own thoughts."

Which approach do you think is the most helpful in overcoming a fear? What empowers you to use a positive approach again?

Why is fear a healthy emotion? It makes you evaluate what you are about to do. It makes you aware of the choices you are about to make and the possible consequences. It's related to the Character Link *I have choices. Choices have consequences.*

How is the Character Link *I enjoy learning* related to *I am courageous*?

Why does taking the first step make you want to continue to learn? (You are encouraged by the good feeling that you get from taking the step you most feared.)

Invite the children to share experiences in which they have shown courage.

35

I HAVE INTEGRITY

35   I HAVE INTEGRITY

Having *integrity* means being completely honest and trustworthy.
It means using all of the Character Links, every day. It means
being a whole and complete person.

Character Links, Character Links,
There seem to be so many!
But master one and then move on
And soon you'll master many.

Chadwick couldn't believe that all the Character Links he had learned led to this moment—the last and final Character Link, *I have integrity.*

While he was learning each of the links, Chadwick learned much about himself. He understood the importance of the links. Each link he learned led to the next link. Every separate link was important. He had grown since he first started, both physically and mentally. In the process of learning the Character Links, Chadwick had become a much wiser kitten.

The journey had been long—difficult and frustrating at times, but very rewarding. The Character Links were part of him now.

Chadwick remembered the lesson he learned in the race with his friend Lettuce the turtle. He constantly worked at keeping an open mind to all the possibilities. He learned to be a good friend, respectful, caring, and responsible. Being trustworthy and honest were essential links to having integrity.

He appreciated and was grateful to everyone who had helped him. Chadwick would reflect on all the lessons as he continued his life's journey. He would use the links every day. He would continue to grow stronger and become a better cat because of the links. One day when he was older, reading stories to kittens, he hoped to be respected and treasured, the way his grandmother was to him.

At Chadwick's graduation, he stood on the rock in the garden holding the last Character Link, the last piece of the puzzle, in his paw. He placed the last piece of the puzzle over his heart. He had integrity. He was whole. He was successful. His mother, grandmother, John Louie, Misifu, Pushpa, Liang, Moo-Moo, Yulan, Pepe, Hedgie, Birdie, Lettuce, and Chipie burst into applause. They all shared his joy.

As part of the celebration, Chadwick's grandmother read a story-poem. She promised to do this as each of the kittens graduated. And this was the story she shared:

A mouse lived in a house
Four stories high
With lots of nooks and crannies and spaces
Over one hundred hiding places.
He played hide and seek with four of the children
Whose shrieks and laughter echoed and bounced throughout
All four stories of
The four story house.
They fed him chunks of cheese,
Petite sweet peas,
Grains and rice and dabs of peanut butter
Until he sputtered
"Enough! Enough! Enough!"
They combed and brushed him
To make his coat shine

Loved and hugged him
All of the time.
At night they put him to bed in the tiniest space ever
Cozy and covered, he fell fast asleep and
Dreamed, during the night
Of delightful new games and limitless fun.
He awakened each morning to breakfast in bed.
Thoughts of exciting new adventures danced through his head.
A luckier, happier mouse never existed

Who lived in a house
Four stories high
With lots of nooks and crannies and spaces
And over one hundred hiding places.

The kittens sighed and thanked Grandma Cat for reading to them. They told her that they were going to their houses to count the nooks and crannies and spaces, hoping to find all the hiding places. How many hiding places do you think they will find?

> After Chadwick had learned all of the Character Links,
> he stood on the rock and said proudly, **"I have integrity!"**

ACTIVITIES

Questions to promote interaction and understanding of this Character Link:

- How did Chadwick feel about arriving at the very last Character Link, *I have integrity*?
- How did he feel he benefited from learning the Character Links?
- How did he feel about each individual link?
- What feelings did he have toward those who had helped him learn the links?
- What were his feelings about his journey?
- How had Lettuce the turtle helped Chadwick to remember the importance of keeping an open mind?
- How was Chadwick going to use the Character Links in his future?
- When he was an older cat reading to kittens, how did he want to be treated?
- When Chadwick stood on the rock and put the last Character Link over his heart, how do you think he felt?
- What do you think Chadwick meant when he stood on the rock and said he was *whole* now?
- When his grandmother celebrated his graduation by reading a poem, how did all the kittens react?

Integrity means being strong enough to do what you know is right. It means knowing the difference between right and wrong and choosing to do the right thing, even when it's difficult.

When Liang stood up for Yulan at school, and told the kittens to STOP teasing Liang, what Character Link was she demonstrating?

When Misifu was honest and told her mother she had broken the plate, what Character Link was she using?

When Chadwick offered part of his lunch to Liang, what Character Link was he demonstrating?

When John Louie stops at a traffic light that is red, and he sees many other cats crossing the street anyway, against the light, he still waits for the green WALK symbol. Is he exhibiting integrity? Why or why not?

Integrity means being the best person you can be. It is a lifelong quest. You will keep learning and experiencing and evaluating and improving every day.